IN THE SHADOW OF THE FALL

ALSO BY TOBI OGUNDIRAN

Jackal, Jackal

TOBI OGUNDIRAN

IN THE SHADOW OF THE FALL

GUARDIAN of the GODS #1

TOR PUBLISHING GROUP
NEW YORK

IN THE SHADOW OF THE FALL

A Tordotcom Book
Published by Tom Doherty Associates / Tor Publishing Group
120 Broadway
New York, NY 10271

www.torpublishinggroup.com

The Library of Congress Cataloging-in-Publication Data
is available upon request.

ISBN 978-1-250-90796-7 (hardcover)
ISBN 978-1-250-90797-4 (ebook)

First Edition: 2024

Printed in the United States of America

0 9 8 7 6 5 4 3 2 1

For my loving siblings,
Ope and Victor,
Mischief Makers and partners in crime

And there arose from among their number,
a man upon whose brow was the sigil of Death,
and in his right hand he held a terrible scimitar,
with which he broke the world.

—Inscription found on a tablet
in the ruins of Ile-Ife

But if it be so that there be no gods, or that they take no care of the world, why should I desire to live in a world void of gods, and of all divine providence?

—Marcus Aurelius, *Meditations*

IN THE SHADOW OF THE FALL

ONE

Alone in the heart of the Sacred Grove, Ashâke lifted her torch and peered into the darkness.

The trees here were old—hundreds of seasons old, their huge white limbs draped in moss. The priests said these trees had been old back when orisha roamed the earth, and still they stood. Ashâke found it hard to shake the feeling of being watched, as she did whenever she came here, and spent a moment wheeling about, straining to see into the darkness beyond the trees. But if there was something there, if there was some*one* there, she couldn't see them.

Ashâke licked her dry lips. *Perhaps it is the orisha who watch me. Waiting for me.* The thought sent chills down her spine. Surely they knew what she was soon to do . . .

She approached the biggest tree, a great white baobab leaning over the river. It stood some eighty feet tall, with bark so wrinkled that it looked like an old, withered face had been carved into it. One could tell a white baobab's age by how many leaves it had left; this one was leafless, limbs oddly naked as they stretched out from a massive trunk. Ashâke dug her torch into the soft soil at its roots. Next to it, she dumped her pouch—which was heavy with her divination board and cowries, and with the tome she'd pilfered from the library, the one that had shown her how to do what she planned.

Ashâke shivered. It was mad, building an idan to summon and bind an orisha. But it was their fault. All their fault for refusing to speak to her, for refusing to *choose* her when they'd chosen her peers, chosen the others.

A gust of wind howled through the forest. Ashâke looked up to see rain clouds lit by intermittent flashes of lightning. *Shango is striking his axes,* she thought. A few heartbeats later, an earsplitting thunderclap cracked through the air, and from somewhere in the forest came the frightened caws of ravens. An omen? Ashâke hoped not. Shango was quick to temper, but it was not him she wanted, not him she sought to summon. She was desperate but had no death wish. Shango would smite her at the first opportunity. She could almost imagine her fellow acolytes, their faces full of wicked derision when they learned of her fate. And the priests, would they tut and shake their heads, muttering about poor Ashâke, whose inability to hear the orisha had driven her to such extremes?

Ashâke gritted her teeth and pushed the voices from her mind. No use dwelling over unfavourable thoughts. She turned her attention to the tree, and the gaping crevice between its roots. It looked ordinary to the casual eye; a bough dammed up with the rot of several seasons, but that was because Ashâke had made it so. Grunting with effort, she began to pull away the dirt—rotted palm fronds, dead leaves and twigs and soil—to reveal—

Eshu, lord of roads and crossroads, messenger orisha, stood before her. His effigy, at least. The greater orisha all had effigies in the temple—towering bronze structures that lined the walls of the Inner Sanctum. But this was no such effigy. For one, it was made of white clay, which Ashâke had painstakingly retrieved from the bottom of the river, diving into the cold water night after night, carefully sifting the riverbed, then stumbling sopping wet through the forest, freezing to her bones as she tried to make it back to the temple before the rousing bell. Moons and moons of dedication had led her to this moment, to the idan before her, carved with the language of binding. And once she performed the final ritual, at last, it would hold Eshu's essence. She would ask her questions, and he would have no choice but to answer.

Why, then, did she hesitate? Why did her hands tremble, her heart flutter? Eshu's blank eyes regarded her, and it seemed to Ashâke that his lips were upturned in the suggestion of a smile.

You're frightened. Simbi's voice rang loud in her head. *What you seek is dangerous. It is not too late to turn back now.*

And then what? Turning back would mean accepting defeat, condemning herself to . . . how many more seasons of ridicule? Her own peers were five seasons into their priesthoods. Yet here she was, stuck as an acolyte, suffering the jeers of the little runts who had come up behind her and now thought themselves her equal.

No. She had to know why the orisha refused to speak to her, where she had gone wrong.

"Ok," she said, taking a deep breath to steel her nerves. "What needs doing must be done well."

Ashâke placed two bundles of loudh in the idan's outstretched hands and lit them. The incense burned, its faintly sweet smoke tickling the back of her throat. Next, she took her knife and drew it across her palm. It stung, and she bit back a whimper as blood bloomed in the fresh cut. Once her hand was full, she poured it over the flames, which hissed, the smoke turning black and pungent, the bitter smell of copper sharp in the back of her throat.

"Eshu Elegba," she intoned. "Messenger lord of the orisha. The one whose path is two hundred and fifty-six. The one whose path is uncountable. I bind you with ashe, which gives me life. I summon you with the breath of Obatala. Come. Come forth."

The wind wailed in the trees, nearly snuffing out the fire. Ashâke waited . . . but nothing happened. Why wasn't it working? The glyphs she'd etched into the effigy should be aglow. Instead, they remained dull white. Ashâke blew out a frustrated breath and squeezed her fist over the fire again, but it had stopped bleeding. She grabbed the bloody dagger, choking back a whimper as she worked it deeper into her palm, until the blood flowed anew, hissing into the flames.

"Eshu Elegba. Messenger lord of the orisha. The one whose path is two hundred and fifty-six; the one whose path is uncountable. I bind you with ashe, which gives me life—"

Her hand moved of its own accord, slamming down on Eshu's outstretched arm. It broke off and tumbled to the ground, the burning loudh snuffing out.

"What—?" She gasped, even as her hand swung for Eshu's second arm. It flew off, spinning fast into the darkness, until it splashed into the river.

She stood there, blinking, struggling to understand what had just happened. A heartbeat passed, then two, then three . . .

The statue erupted in flames.

Ashâke yelped, leaping backwards. She tripped on a root and flailed desperately to stop her fall. Twisting at the last moment, she landed with such jarring force that her jaw snapped shut and arrows of pain shot up her arms. She howled. The entire sculpture was ablaze, the flames climbing high, high, licking the great white baobab. It was an unnatural fire, and in it she saw—

She saw a burning hall, every inch of it wreathed in golden flames. She saw a table, and seated behind it were shadows, voids in the shape of men, which even the raging fire did not consume. She heard voices, all of them speaking her name, calling her. Hands reached out of the dark, grasped at her, seeking to wrench her apart. Ashâke felt *stretched,* as though there were things in her head, things that *shouldn't* be there.

"STOP!" she screamed. "STOP! I'M SORRY!"

She pushed to her feet and fled, running from the voices, from the things grasping at her. She had overreached. Who was she in her hubris to bind an orisha? Now she had angered Eshu, angered them all, and the orisha were nothing if not vindictive in their vengeance.

The ground vanished beneath her, and then she was falling, tumbling head over heels down the steep riverbank, slamming again and again into the slope. She splashed into the water, cracking her head on a gnarled root.

The darkness took her.

TWO

A thin face leaned over her. An old, crusty patch covered the left eye, while the other one appraised her with mild curiosity. And out of a thatch of grey-white goat beard stuck a moonleaf pipe like a branch. A curious face, but it was one Ashâke would recognise anywhere.

"Hem. Good evening." Ba Fatai, the witch doctor, frowned. "Although it is two hours past midnight and even the owls have gone silent. So I must wish you good morning."

Ashâke moaned, trying to sit up.

"Yah!—don't try to move just yet," he cried, pressing her back to the bed with bony hands. "We don't want your brain rattling loose, although you must already be severely lacking in that regard. That is the only explanation for what you've done."

She was in pain. So much pain. Her head throbbed where she had cracked it against that root, and the bandage Ba Fatai had wrapped around it only seemed to make it worse. It felt like a couple of malevolent egbere had taken their little hammers to the inside of her skull. She reached up to ease the tightness of the bandage and Ba Fatai slapped her hand away.

"Don't move, I said." The witch doctor plucked the pipe from his mouth and offered it to her. "For the pain. Have three puffs."

Ashâke sucked on the pipe, smoke filling her mouth and lungs. She managed two puffs before she burst into a racking cough, and the egbere renewed their hammering.

"Water," she croaked.

Ba Fatai vanished, returning moments later with a cup of water. It dribbled down her chin as she drank greedily. Once she'd slaked her thirst she sank back to the bed, sighing.

She was in the witch doctor's quarters. She couldn't remember the last time she had come here—perhaps when she had been thirteen seasons and had eaten some poison mushrooms with Simbi—but the same wooden masks still hung from the walls, their sunken eyes scowling down at her; the same bronze-and-pewter cauldrons still bubbled with concoctions, their vapours, not to mention the ungodly stench of moonleaves, choking the air so that she felt as if she were suffocating. Ashâke wondered if the fires ever went out; it seemed the witch doctor was always preparing one potion or the other.

She had thought she was dead.

"Who . . . who found me?" she asked, her voice hoarse.

"Who do you think? In all my seasons I have met many a foolish acolyte, but you, my dear, you are the most foolish of all." He huffed. "The orisha must favour you. I was out collecting moonleaves when I found you—heard you screaming, more like. A most curious thing, eh? Because you see, moonleaves do not grow in the part of the woods where I found you. I knew that, and still I went there. And I *never* walk that part of the woods." He glowered at her through his one good eye. "Why is that? Why don't I walk that part of the woods?"

Ashâke swallowed, looked away. "Because it is the Sacred Grove," she mumbled. "Only the priests and High Priestess go there."

"Ah. And here I was thinking you were green. Turns out you're just daft."

Daft, desperate, angry. It all depended on how you looked at it. Ashâke waited for the question: What had she been doing there? If Ba Fatai had pulled her out of the water, then he must have seen the blazing statue, must have seen the knife and her pouch with the stolen tome . . .

His eye travelled slowly to the empty pouch sitting on the table, then back to her. "Aye," he growled. "Just daft."

At that moment there came a knock on the door. Ba Fatai pushed up from his stool with a grunt and hobbled towards the door, vanishing behind the curtain of beads. The slide of a bolt, creak of hinges; and then hushed voices. Ashâke tried to listen but could not make out the voices, but she didn't have to think hard to guess who they were or what they wanted.

"They want you," said Ba Fatai some moments later as he reentered the chamber. "The priests, that is. They are like hounds at a feast, but I have kept them away, for now."

"Thank you," she mumbled.

"Rest," he grunted. "There'll be trouble come morning."

Trouble did not wait for morning. The door rattled in its frame as someone hammered on it. Once, twice, thrice. Ashâke sat up, jolted from her moonleaf stupor.

"Coming! I'm coming!" yelled Ba Fatai, flinging a spatula on the worktable. It skidded across, knocking over a small decanter that spilled its black contents on the floor. He swore.

The knock came again. Louder. Harder.

"Orisha take you! That door is not a drum!"

No sooner had he opened the door than Priestess Essie pushed her way into the room, nostrils flared as her eyes searched for Ashâke. She wore a white raiment, three loops of coral beads, which marked her as a senior priestess, choking her neck, her hair pulled back in severe braids that stretched her eyebrows over her forehead.

"She is not yet recovered," said Ba Fatai, pushing to block her path.

"She looks well enough to me," said the priestess. "Well enough to answer my questions."

"She is in no fit state to *move*. I am yet to ascertain if she bleeds inside her head. Any errant movement, emotional excitement, and she could drop dead—"

"*If* she drops dead," said Essie, biting off each word, "it will be because she brought it on herself."

Silence followed her words, broken only by the gurgle of Ba Fatai's many potions.

"Leave, Priestess," Ba Fatai growled. "The acolyte is in my care, and as such, is my ward. You cannot take her."

The priestess's eyebrows climbed even higher. "Would you deny the High Priestess? Would you have me tell the Mother of Mysteries that *you denied* her?"

The High Priestess? *Shit.* Ashâke, in all her twenty-two seasons at the temple, could count on one finger the number of times she had seen the High Priestess. The woman rarely left the Inner Sanctum and did not seem to concern herself with the daily workings of the temple—that was more Priestess Essie's domain. Ashâke knew she was in trouble, would have to answer for what she had done. But to have the High Priestess personally summon her? That did not bode well. She wondered if now was a good time to pretend to faint.

"Well, obviously," said Ba Fatai, "I'm not denying the High—"

"Then I suggest you step aside and return to your"—she cast about the chamber, an expression of thinly veiled disdain on her face—"*concoctions* and leave matters of import to priests. Yes?" Without waiting for an answer, she turned to Ashâke. "You. With me. Now."

Ashâke looked at Ba Fatai but he shrugged. There would be no more help from him. He had done all he could. She pushed to her feet, staggered as the room wobbled around her, then shuffled out, the priestess in her wake.

Through the high windows of the corridor Ashâke saw the ink-black sky was already giving way to the azure of morning. The halls were empty, and as they marched across, it was hard not to feel as though she were walking towards her death. Her punishment would be swift and severe, there was no doubt about that. It was the uncertainty of the nature of punishment that worried her. She hadn't simply broken curfew to engage in a midnight tryst; she had built an idan. Attempted to call and bind an orisha. It would have all been worth it had she succeeded, had she finally been able to speak with one of them. Instead, she . . . no. She didn't want to think about it.

They passed through a courtyard where two acolytes on morning duty were leaning against their brooms, snoozing. Essie barked at them and they leapt into action, mumbling as they swept up dust and fallen leaves from the stone floor.

Soon they stopped before the massive double doors that led into the Grand Hall.

"Enter."

Ashâke entered. The Hall was vast, its sides curving gently up into a dome that let in light from above. The walls were an undulating sheet of sculptures rendered in bas-relief: it told a tale of the making of the world—from when Obatala first cast a bowlful of sand into the Endless Sea to create the continent, to the making of the first peoples, to the construction of the Tower of the Orisha that connected Aye to Orun. Sometimes when sunlight hit at the right angle it seemed the walls came alive, the scenes transformed from static images caught in stone to living, breathing things. It was Ashâke's favourite place in the temple, and the one place she felt closest to the orisha.

At the centre of the hall, five chairs were arranged in a semicircle. Ashâke's heart sank at the sight of the seated figures: on the far right sat a harried-looking Priest Jegede, conversing in low tones with Priest Dunsin; opposite them sat Priestess Tokunbo, the seat next to her empty. And at the head of the semicircle, Iyalawo, the High Priestess. She was garbed in midnight blue, her face hidden behind a bronze mask. Never had Ashâke, or anyone that she knew of for that matter, glimpsed the face behind that mask. The acolytes whispered it was because she was not wholly mortal and had the essence of an orisha coursing through her veins. Whatever it was, an indescribable aura surrounded the High Priestess, and the mask only added to her air of mystique.

Priestess Essie swept towards the chairs, inclined her head in deference to the High Priestess, then settled into her seat.

Silence ensued as five pairs of eyes regarded Ashâke. To think that mere hours ago she had been just one among hundreds of acolytes, not particularly worthy of any special attention, if one ignored the painful fact that she had failed for five seasons in a row to accede to the priesthood. And now, now the most senior priests were gathered because of her in the small hours of the morning.

Priestess Essie cleared her throat as she leaned forwards. "The binding of—"

Priest Dunsin broke abruptly into a hacking cough, one that continued for a painful minute and left him gasping for breath.

Priestess Essie glowered at him. "Would the priest . . . like to be excused?"

"No, no," he gasped, waving one hand while he fumbled in his raiment with the other. Producing a kerchief, he hawked into it, frowned at the contents, then folded it away. "Rain season. Does things to my lungs. Carry on, carry on . . ."

Priestess Essie turned back to Ashâke. "The summoning and binding of orisha is an archaic ritual, one even seasoned priests know little of, much less attempt. Where did you learn of this? Where did you learn to do this?"

Ashâke swallowed. *I broke into the library's restricted section, stole a book, and copied it word for word.* But she couldn't tell them that. She was in enough trouble as it was.

"Acolyte!" Priestess Essie's voice cracked like a whip. "You will speak when spoken to! Where did you learn of the binding?"

Ashâke cleared her throat. "Em . . . I cannot say, Priestess."

"You *cannot—*?" Priestess Essie's eyes looked like they would fall from their sockets. "Do you think this is some jape, or that you can choose not to answer my questions? Do you not understand the severity of your plight?"

"I do, Priestess," said Ashâke. "And I meant no disrespect. It is just—I cannot say where I learned of the binding because I do not remember."

"You do not remember?"

"Yes. When I . . . fell, I hit my head and . . . it's hard to remember some things."

It was a lie of course, and the look on the priestess's face said she did not believe a word, knew that Ashâke was lying. But there was no way to prove it, after all she *had* taken a fall, and hit her head . . .

"I see . . ." said Priestess Essie.

"I'm sorry, Priestess. Much of my memory is a blur."

The priestess blew out a frustrated breath, jowls quivering. "Is there *anything* you do remember?"

Fire. The voices. The hands. "Falling. I remember falling."

The priestess sank back into her seat, her bosom heaving. "No matter," she said with icy calm. "Let me help jog your memory: you were caught breaking curfew. You were found desecrating the Sacred Grove. You built an idan and botched an attempt to call and bind an orisha—one that led to the burning and subsequent death of a sacred tree. You gave no thoughts to your actions—perhaps you did, and simply did not care. You endangered not only yourself but also the lives of us all here in the temple. Lastly, and most importantly, you have as yet to show any remorse." Priestess Essie inhaled deeply, turning to the other priests. "Anathema. That is what I propose. That she be banished from this temple, lest she be a corrupting influence on the acolytes. That she be shunned by all the priests across the Ten Kingdoms. The orisha evidently have no use for her, and neither should we."

"No!" Ashâke cried, dropping to her knees. "Please—"

"You will speak only when spoken to and no more!"

The tears came unbidden to her eyes and she scrubbed at them. They couldn't . . . they couldn't possibly mean to banish her. Not after all these seasons of service. She, like every other acolyte, had been brought here as a child. She couldn't remember a life outside these walls, couldn't even remember her own parents! She knew nothing else. Leaving here without attaining priesthood would be more than a disgrace. Her life would have no purpose. This was a fate worse than death.

"I was desperate!" she cried.

"I said—" Essie began.

"Let her speak," said Tokunbo. "Let us hear what the acolyte has to say."

She had promised herself never to do this, never to let anyone see how much pain and shame her situation caused her. Hadn't she endured the endless taunts and whispers? Yet here she was, on her knees, pleading for a life in the temple, a life of service, however tortured it was. Ashâke was filled with a profound sense of shame, but she forced herself to look at each priest, meeting their eyes in turn. "I am two and twenty seasons. I should have acceded five seasons ago. You all know this. What you don't know—what you *cannot* know is how it feels to be the only acolyte to be shunned by the orisha, to wonder again and again what you did to deserve this. I have done everything, studied more, I daresay, than any other acolyte. I have dedicated myself to service. There is nothing more I want than to serve the orisha, but I cannot do that if they won't speak to me!"

How many times had she stood in this very hall, watching first her peers, then her juniors enter the Inner Sanctum and emerge as priests? How many times had she abased herself before the orisha's effigies, hoping, *praying* that they choose her? How many times had she walked away, unable to shake the niggling feeling that there was something terribly wrong with her? "I only sought to know, to ask why . . ." She sniffed, wiping her eyes. "It was foolish of me; I know that and I'm so sorry, but *please* . . . you cannot turn me away."

Silence.

"Even now," said Priestess Essie icily, "she presumes to tell us what we can and cannot do."

"Come now," said Priest Jegede. "We cannot turn her away. She is not acceded. You know we don't set acolytes loose upon the world—and for good reason. And, well . . ." He frowned at Ashâke, tugging his beard. "She might have gone about it the wrong way, but her intentions were pure—"

"Pure?" cried the priestess, as though that was the most ridiculous word ever uttered. "Need I *remind* you that she endangered the lives of everyone in the temple? You all saw the idan. It wasn't built in a day! Which means she stole out *night* after *night*. Why, she could have met with any of—of *them*. How do we know the followers—"

"Priestess Essie," warned Priestess Tokunbo.

The priests fell into a charged silence as they exchanged meaningful looks. There was something they were not saying, something they clearly did not want to bring to light in her hearing.

The followers.

But what followers? Was that what had them all worried, that she might have learned of the binding from . . . someone? But from who?

Acolytes were forbidden from leaving the temple unless accompanied by a priest. Ostensibly to keep them focused on their service. But what if it was also to protect them? What if Ashâke, in her quest to hear the orisha, had truly endangered them all?

Fire. Voices. Hands.

Priest Dunsin turned his rheumy eyes on Ashâke. "Was there ever anyone else . . . out there with you?"

"No!" cried Ashâke, shaking her head. "It was just me. I swear it."

"I thought you did not remember," said Priestess Essie. "Or you do, now. Which is it?"

"I . . ."

"What happened?" It was the High Priestess who spoke. They all fell silent and turned to stare at her. "What happened when you performed the ritual?"

"I . . ." Ashâke mouthed wordlessly. "It didn't work. The . . . the idan went up in flames and . . . my sleeve caught fire and I tried to beat it off."

"Leave us," said Iyalawo.

It took Ashâke a moment to realise who that had been directed at.

"Mother of Mysteries . . ." Priestess Essie began, but her protests died when that bronze mask turned on her. She dipped her head. "As you command."

The priests pushed out of their chairs, bowing their heads before filing out of the hall. Priest Dunsin's hacking cough took him, even beyond the double doors.

"Come closer, child."

Ashâke pushed to her feet and moved forward two strides so that she could see the High Priestess's eyes glittering behind that mask.

"When I was a girl," said Iyalawo, "many seasons ago—much younger than you are now, I fell off a cliff and into rapids. I was convinced I was going to die. And as the water pulled me under, as death rushed into my lungs, I cried out to any orisha who was listening to help me. To save me. One did. The orisha are always listening. They may not speak to you, but they're always listening." She paused. "I understand how you feel. Lost, without direction. But perhaps it is for a reason."

"Forgive me, but I fail to see the reason."

"I know." Iyalawo rose to her feet and closed the distance between them. "Now, I will ask you a question, and I want you to think carefully before answering."

"Yes, High Priestess."

"What did you see, when you performed the ritual?"

INTERLUDE I

Yaruddin

The city of Skaggás accosted Yaruddin as he stepped off the boat. It stank of fish and night soil and the rank stench of humanity. Hundreds of stalls had sprouted up on the road leading away from the docks, each seller trying to outshout the other as they bellowed about their wares at freshly arrived travellers. The din was maddening and Yar longed to quiet them. But that would draw too much attention, and if there was one thing the Teacher taught them, it was to never draw attention.

Yar allowed the throng to sweep him off the docks and into the city proper. He remembered a time when it had been little more than a hamlet, a measly collection of hovels lurking in the shadow of the Skaggási mountains, the small folk subsisting on what they could barter from their cane sugar farms; now broad thoroughfares lined the city, buildings of stone and baked earth towering high into the sky. This was not the Skaggás Yar remembered. But then, the world had changed a lot since the Fall.

The deeper into the city he ventured, the more he felt the pulse, a subtle tugging in his chest like a beacon calling to him. He had felt it ever since he had roused from slumber, and it allowed him to know the location of his brothers and sisters scattered across the Ten Kingdoms and beyond.

"You need a room, baba? A place to eat? A whore? I know all the good places here. Cheap too."

A youth of no more than thirteen seasons had fallen into step with him. He had the hungry look of an urchin, the sunken but bright eyes that told of a life spent scavenging on the streets. His dashiki was many sizes too small so that he looked like an insect stuffed into a sack. Yar frowned at the pendant around his scrawny neck, a crudely carved effigy of a hunter and a dog: the symbol of Ogun.

"I will require a room," said Yar.

The boy flashed a grin and nodded. "Come with me, baba."

Evening was fast falling, and the denizens of Skaggás flooded the streets, some clustering about smoking suya stands, others flocking to taverns. Yar struggled to keep up, and the boy kept looking impatiently over his shoulder, dark eyes sweeping the street as he urged him on. He was leading Yar in a direction opposite to the pulse, so that with each stride he felt the tugging a little less.

"What is your name, boy?"

The youth frowned in suspicion. "What's it to you?"

"You do me a great favour, the least I can do is thank you properly."

He seemed to consider it a moment, then shrugged. "Vig."

"Thank you, Vig."

He grunted, ushering him ahead. "It is just round the corner."

Yar stepped into the alley, which was really a narrow space between two shanties, whose grimy walls were crawling with wet moss and poorly disposed night soil. A wreckage of old furniture and broken wagon wheels blocked the alley.

"Should've saved that thanks for later, eh?" he heard Vig sneer behind him. "I'll take that sack, old man."

Yar turned around to find Vig blocking his path, a dagger at hand. "Are we alone?"

"Yes. No one will hear you scream, old man."

Yar smiled. "Good. Very good."

Vig frowned, as though he could not quite comprehend why Yar was not responding the way he expected. "Do you want to die, old man?" His voice climbed a register. "Drop the sack and fuck off 'fore I open your guts—"

He squealed as Yar seized him, locking one arm under his armpit and twisting the other until he let go of the knife and it dropped to the ground with a clatter. Then Yar slammed the boy into the wall, pinning him by the neck. He started to whimper, eyes rolling like a spooked horse's.

"Thank you, Vig," Yar said softly.

"Wait—what are you—?"

"For this gift of your body."

Most bodies, Yar took without warning or preamble.

Rarely did he grant his prey the grace to know what was coming. And for those he did grant, they never quite *understood* exactly what it was.

"Please." Tears leaked down Vig's grimy cheeks. "Just let me go. I'm sorry . . . *please*."

"In the name of the Teacher," Yar muttered, then Ate him.

Ashe was an endless thing, the life force that thrummed through every living entity, from the birds of the air to the trees of the forest. And as Yar's spirit rushed out of his body and into Vig's, he saw the boy's ashe, a pale ball of light flickering about almost . . . almost like a firefly. Yar rushed towards it, consuming it until there was nothing left of the boy, so it was as though he had never existed and could not be reincarnated. The boy's memories still remained, trace vestiges of a life that was, that *could* have been. In any other case Yar might have kept them, the better to blend in, but there was no need. The boy would not be missed. So he discarded the memories and released himself, taking his new body like bronze filling the shape of a new cast.

Yar opened his eyes to find the old man's hand still wrapped around his throat. He pushed him away, and the lifeless body crumpled to the floor. He was taken aback at the sight of the old man: the sparse white hair and deep lined skin, shrivelled like dried fruit. A body was simply a thing to be worn and discarded once it had outlived usefulness, like an old frayed kaftan. Yar still remembered taking that body, coming upon the lone farmhouse and the farmer. He had kept the man's memories, lived with his family until he could no longer mask his slow ageing, and then he'd simply gotten up one night and walked away. That had been in the beginning, many seasons ago, when he'd still wrestled with conflicting emotions. Yar searched himself for any trace of remorse and found none. Such base emotions were beyond him now. There was only the work. There was only service to the Teacher, and he would see that to its end.

His clothes were tight. He would have to find himself some new ones. Yar snatched the pendant from his neck and crushed it in one fist, letting the wind carry away the dust. Then he collected his sack from where it had fallen and turned to leave.

Three urchins stood at the mouth of the alley, gaping in frozen horror. Vig's cronies, no doubt. This was where they lured their victims and divvied up their spoils.

"Vig is no more," Yar said. "Go."

They looked in his eyes and did not see anything they recognised.

"Go," he repeated.

They scattered, hyenas fleeing before lions.

Yar let them go, repressing the urge to give chase. Killing them served no purpose. And besides, he was not unkind.

Always, let gentle mercy temper the fires of your wrath, the Teacher taught. *In that, there is balance.*

Through the dusty shop windows, Yar made out rows and rows of crockery and terra-cotta sculptures. Above, scrawled on the hanging sign, were the words: MASTER VASHEK'S MARVELLOUS CROCKERY. Yar crossed the street and entered the shop, the bell over the door announcing his presence.

The shop was cramped, the already sparse foot space given to several shelves, each of which teetered under the weight of glazed and intricately decorated earthenware. So delicately arranged they were that it seemed even the slightest breath of wind would send the whole arrangement crashing to the floor.

A bald man of about forty seasons sat at a table, whittling at a piece of wood. Vashek. He had been wearing a different body when last they met. He frowned as he worked, the lantern light washing off his pate. Dark patches of sweat stuck out on his white kaftan.

A young woman stood in the corner, wiping down some cups with a flywhisk. She looked up at Yar's approach and frowned. "This is no place for street rats," she said. "Away with you."

"It's alright, Bilkis," said Vashek, without looking up. "I'm expecting him."

She eyed Yar. "Are you sure, Papa?"

"Please. Leave us."

She looked like she would argue, but then sighed. She untied her apron and hung it on a nail in the back of the shop. "I'm going to prepare supper. Lock up, will you, Papa? And don't forget to latch the windows. You always do." She kissed him on his pate and scurried out of the shop.

Yar stood some five paces from Vashek, watching him work.

"You took too long."

"Forgive me, Vashek," said Yar. "I came as quickly as I could, but the wind blew westward, and my boatman was an inexperienced lad."

Vashek held the figurine up to the light, blew at it. "Come. Sit."

Yar took the stool opposite him.

"You will go south."

"What lies south?"

"Three nights ago a ripple passed through the world. It was there for only the briefest of moments, but I felt it. Felt them."

Yar sat forward, his heart hammering in excitement. "You found them."

"Not quite. But I know *where* we should be looking. After all this time, I feared that they were regrouping, biding their time. But no. If anything they are . . . weaker."

"Weaker." Yar turned the word in his mouth, and found that he liked the taste. "That is good. That is very good."

"Yes," Vashek agreed. "But weakened or not, they still elude us."

"We will find them. And if this search proves unfruitful, we can always reveal ourselves. If the people of the Ten Kingdoms—"

Vashek stopped whittling and fixed him with a gaze that could burn. "No," he said, slowly shaking his head. "No, no, no. Have you learned nothing?" He placed his hands on the table. "When you strike a goat, over and over again, in a bid to stop it from eating your vegetables, it doesn't. Why?"

"Because it is a goat?"

"Because that is its source of sustenance. Or so it believes. And no matter what obstacles you place in its path, no matter how hard you beat it, it *will* continue to eat your vegetables." Vashek leaned forward, the table groaning beneath his weight. "But take away the vegetables. Better yet, weave the illusion that there, in that beloved patch of garden, no longer lies sustenance but a barren stretch of ground, and the goat will of its own accord cease to go there. It will look to other places for food. This is what we do. We weave the illusion, until it becomes truth: a subtly placed word, whispered in the dark, goes a long way to erode their resolve, their faith. And when the people turn to seek sustenance elsewhere, there will we be, the followers of Bahl'ul, waiting with open arms to welcome them among us."

Vashek appraised him, then handed him what he had

been carving. It was a figurine of the Teacher. "You must believe in the Teacher."

"I do."

"You must trust in His designs."

"I do."

"Good. The end is nigh, I can feel it. We will yet prevail."

A few moments later, Yaruddin stepped out of the shop and into the sweltering night, glad to be on the hunt again.

THREE

The rat was a starved thing, eyes gleaming like black beads in the lantern light, whole stretches of wrinkled skin visible where its coat had fallen out. Ashâke remained perfectly still as it climbed onto her hard cot and padded along her leg to where her dinner lay uneaten. The rats down here were bold and would gnaw the finger off your hand if they could.

"Don't mind if you do," Ashâke whispered as the rat helped itself to her meal of sweetcorn and bean stew.

She had no appetite, had not had one in the two—or was it three?—days she'd been here. Bloody hell. Already she was starting to feel unmoored, lost without the solid pace of routine, however much she had detested it, to ground her. She marked the passing of time by the frequency of her meals and how often they refilled her lantern with oil. She sighed, resting her head against the wall. After much deliberation the priests had agreed that she should not be sent away—to Ashâke's great relief—but neither should she be allowed to go unpunished, to slip back into routine as though nothing had transpired. So they'd sentenced her to a fortnight of isolation, for her to contemplate her folly. Still, it was saying something that there were no dungeons in the temple, and Ashâke had to be kept down here in the abandoned larder with the dark and the rats for company.

The larder was a vast warren of alcoves beneath the kitchens, and Ashâke was generally free to roam its length. The first thing she had done was investigate if there were other exits, but she had found none. There was just the one—the arched door that led to the kitchens, whose iron key hung around the cook's neck.

Ashâke sometimes fancied she could hear acolytes above her. She hated the shifts she pulled in the kitchen, dicing tubers or pounding yams, labouring over bubbling pots in the heat, not to mention the cook, Priestess Wunmi, yelling at them about salt or curry or some other such condiment. Now she would gladly take a shift in the kitchen if it meant escaping this blasted place.

The High Priestess's question still burned in Ashâke's mind: *What did you see when you performed the ritual?*

Ashâke had thought of lying, but Iyalawo's question had been specific, urgent. She was searching for something.

"I saw a hall, and it was on fire," said Ashâke, shuddering at the thought. "I heard voices calling my name. Someone—several someones tried to grab me."

Iyalawo was silent. Ashâke had the disquieting feeling that there was something the High Priestess was waiting to hear.

"What does it mean?" she asked.

"It means you courted with things you do not understand, and we should all count ourselves lucky that you were not successful."

That was not an answer, but Ashâke had come to expect prevarication. Priests and their numerous secrets. It only served to confirm that things were being kept from her, and she itched to know what they were.

Maybe some things are not meant for you to be knowing, Simbi told her. *That's how you got yourself into trouble in the first place.*

Ashâke sighed, sinking back onto her cot. She missed Simbi, missed her dearly. Simbi had been her one friend. Now she was gone, a priestess of Yemoja, out somewhere in the Ten Kingdoms serving her orisha.

"What was I supposed to do, wait indefinitely on the orisha until they deigned to pay me any mind? I can't just—"

"Talking to ourselves, are we?" said a bright voice.

"Ba Fatai," Ashâke sat up, "I didn't hear you come."

"No, you didn't," said the witch doctor, settling his medicine bag on the table. His kutu flew off his shoulder and landed on Ashâke's head. "Alright, let me see that hand."

He unwrapped the now filthy bandage, exposing her wound. A deep angry gash went from the base of her little finger to just beneath her thumb. It was healing, if slowly, congealed black blood starting to harden around the stitch and form a scab. Bits of bandage were trapped in it, and Ba Fatai plucked them out with a long needle. Then he began to pull out the old stitching, working the sharp point of the needle just under the newly growing skin to unravel it. It stung quite a bit, but not as sharply as when the cut had been fresh. "This is healing quite well," Ba Fatai remarked. "Can't say the same for your state of mind."

Ashâke sighed. "I wasn't talking to myself."

"To spirits and ghosts, then?"

"No, it was my . . . it's just something I do to help me think." She hated that she had to explain herself. "I haven't . . . gone mad."

Ba Fatai cocked his one eyebrow. "I don't believe I called you mad." He turned to the bird. "Did I call her mad?"

"No," said the kutu.

"You *insinuated*—"

Ba Fatai gave a low chuckle. "Young lady, I do not insinuate. That is the coward's way. To hint and dance around the issue, using flowery phrases where one word will suffice. Hem! *I* simply say as it is. For example: you smell awful. You smell like something abominable died and clawed out of its grave—"

"I've not had a bath in days!" cried Ashâke, her neck suddenly warm. "I have to *shit* in a pail!"

"And whose fault is that?"

Ashâke blew out a frustrated breath. Her fault. All her fault. It was bad enough that she had gotten used to the smell, both of her sweat and her shit, but to be reminded of it, the humiliation was more than she could bear.

Ba Fatai grinned at her, evidently enjoying himself. He reached into his medicine bag and produced a gourd of fermented palm wine. He took a swig, throat stone bobbing, then poured the rest over her hand to wash the wound. "There," he said. "I won't wrap it this time. We have to let it breathe."

"Thank you," said Ashâke.

"Here." He grunted, then reached into his bag and produced a small ball of pressed moonleaves, which he gave to her. "For chewing." She took it gingerly, turning it slowly in her hand. Ashâke looked from the ball to Ba Fatai, who was now gathering his tools, stuffing the needle and thread and soiled bandage into his bag. Then she stared at the piece of cloth wrapped around his unseeing left eye.

"How did you find me?" she asked. "In the Grove."

He frowned at her. "I told you this, I think. Or are you losing your memory too?"

"You were collecting moonleaves, but . . . you said you never go into the Grove—no one does, so what prompted you to go there that night?"

He shrugged. "Just count yourself lucky I was there to pull you out the water."

Ashâke popped the ball into her mouth. It was bitter. "I think you saw me."

"Not at first." He grinned at her. "'Twas your piggish squeals what I heard."

"Piggish squeals," echoed the kutu.

"No," said Ashâke, picking her words carefully. "Not on that day, perhaps not even the day before, but you *saw* me . . . you saw with your White Eye."

Ba Fatai froze. He still knelt before Ashâke, head bowed, his hand hovering over the clasp of his bag. He remained unmoving for a time, then slowly he raised his head to regard her. Ashâke could feel her heart thudding in her throat. Had she misjudged? Was he simply just . . . blind and wore the patch to hide it? But then the witch doctor broke into a hard smile. "You *are* clever," he said softly, and the playfulness was gone from his voice. "Much cleverer than you're given credit for."

If she had not been sitting, she would have collapsed to the cot. She was right. Obatala's breath, she was right. It had been a guess, a wild gamble, but her suspicions were true!

Priests of Divinity were rare as thunderstones. Orunmila was infamously picky with whom he bestowed his favour, and it was said that he chose his priests once every hundred seasons. Here was Ba Fatai, whom she had thought of all her life as nothing more than a witch doctor, but was in truth a priest of Divinity!

"You . . . you have the Sight," she croaked.

"I do."

"So you *did* see me."

"Many seasons ago. I saw myself pull you out of that river."

Ashâke felt suddenly cold.

"I don't understand," she said. "Why do you pretend that you're not a priest? Why be a lowly witch doctor?"

"Pretend? I do not pretend. Once I was a priest; now I am a witch doctor."

Slowly, Ba Fatai unwrapped the patch to reveal the Eye, white as hard-boiled egg and threaded with blood vessels, growing like tree roots, branching and connecting until there was only one spot of white at the very centre. The eye did not see, not in the way a normal eye did, and it was disconcerting to look at it. Ashâke felt as though it bored into the very depths of her soul, like it saw all of her. Above the eye, in the arch where his eyebrow should be, were glyphs cut into his very flesh. And even though she could not read them, it was not hard to guess what they meant. After all, she had carved something similar into the idan.

"You *bound* your Eye?" she whispered. This was something she would do anything to have, something she *had* gone over and beyond to have: the favour of the orisha, the honour of having one of them choose you, speak to you. And Ba Fatai had more than that. Perhaps this was why Priestess Essie regarded him with such contempt. He had been given a gift, a rare gift at that, and he'd spat in the face of the orisha. Spat in the face of Orunmila.

"Why would you *do* that? How could you turn your back on your service?"

"Easily."

"Easily?" She struggled to understand. "But *why*?"

"There is no greater burden than to know what is to come," said Ba Fatai. "To be powerless to stop it. You are not shown the future to alter it, because you cannot. You may try, you may delay it, but the future will be made manifest. Those of us gifted with the White Eye are simply observers, there to record prophecies and nothing more." He shook his head. "To glimpse the future is not a gift. It is a curse."

"A curse," echoed the kutu.

"My predecessor, Olayaki, the greatest priest of Divinity to ever live, looked too far and too long into the future. And it drove him mad." Ba Fatai's lips peeled back in a snarl. "Some look so long into the future that they cannot tell what is present and what is yet to come. Their mind becomes warped, stretched across a thousand seasons. The mortal mind is not made to know so much; that way lies madness, and I will not go down that path. Why bother, when it is all pointless?"

Ashâke swallowed, looking at Ba Fatai. Even his kutu had stopped flapping, fixing her with a bloodred stare. He rewrapped the cloth around the White Eye.

"Do you know my future? What will become of me? Will I . . . will I ever hear the orisha? Will they choose me?"

Ba Fatai looked at her long and hard. "I don't know."

"You're lying."

He glowered at her, then turned to leave.

"Please!" Ashâke cried, grabbing his sleeve. "Please, if you know something you must tell me. You *have* to!"

"I said I do not know."

"Then look into my future," she said. "I beg you."

Ba Fatai cursed. "Did you not hear a word of what I said, or are you just dense?"

"I did, but . . . I *have* to know. It's the least I deserve."

"Deserve?" he growled, lips peeling back to show yellow teeth. "*Deserve?* You know nothing of the world. How can you, when the walls of this temple have defined your life? We do not deserve anything except that which is our lot. We take that and we must be content with it."

"Is my lot then to not hear the orisha?"

"The orisha keep their own counsel, acolyte, except when they don't. If they do not wish to speak to you, if they want nothing to do with you, then there is little I can do."

He yanked free of her grip so violently that she stumbled forwards and sprawled to the floor, cracking her jaw on the hard floor. Blood filled her mouth, hot and salty. For a moment the witch doctor looked like he would stoop to help her up, for a moment he looked like he would say something. But then he spun abruptly on his heels and walked away, his kutu flapping after him.

Up the steps and out the larder he went, the door slamming shut behind him, plunging Ashâke once more into darkness.

FOUR

Ashâke spent the next few days preparing her argument for when Ba Fatai returned to check on her hand. But when the days drew on, she began to wonder if he would return. Her hand was healing nicely, so she reopened the wound and when next her meal was brought, she showed it to the acolyte and asked for Ba Fatai. She was snoozing when she heard the ruffle of feathers and started awake.

Ba Fatai's kutu was perched next to the lantern on her table, watching her with beady red eyes. The light washed over its red-and-orange plumage so it seemed as though it were ablaze.

"How did you get in here?" She cast around, expecting to see Ba Fatai, but the larder was empty. "Where is your master?"

"Gone," said the kutu.

"Gone? What do you mean gone?"

"I have a message for you." A ripple passed through the bird, and it spoke in Ba Fatai's voice. "You're clinging to a path that is not yours."

". . . what?"

"You wanted to know your future: you do not belong to this temple. There is nothing for you here."

Silence, as Ashâke digested these words.

"You're lying," she said. "Please, tell me you're lying."

The bird said nothing.

Ashâke rose to unsteady feet, wincing as she placed her weight on her injured hand. "What of the orisha?" she whispered. "Will they . . . will they speak to me?" It could be that she did not belong in the temple, that her future was not here. After all, when acolytes acceded, they were sent into the world to do as they pleased. Some went on to join other temples; others, like Simbi, like Ashâke herself had planned, remained in the cities as advisors to kings, helpers to the poor, mediators for the common man.

"I cannot say."

Tears stung Ashâke's eyes. This was it, then. She had reached the end. Even if it had meant remaining in the temple for several more seasons, enduring ridicule and contempt and pity, she would have gladly done it, sure in the knowledge that at the end she would get her reward. But now . . . now Ba Fatai was saying the orisha did not want her. That they had rejected her.

"Why?" Ashâke whispered, swaying on her feet. She wiped angrily at her tears. "Why? All I'm ever served are riddles from priests and silence from orisha. How is that fair? I never asked for this life. I never asked to be torn away from my parents and brought into service. But that is what happened, and it became what I wanted to do. It is all I know and . . . they won't even let me do that! What did I ever do to deserve this? Why can't I just *be* like others? Why?"

"You are clinging to a path that is not yours," the kutu repeated. It could say nothing more, nor offer her any advice. It had been tasked to deliver a message, and its work was done.

"Damn them." She said it quietly, as tears poured down her cheeks. And then she began to scream: "DAMN THE ORISHA! DAMN EVERY SINGLE ONE OF THEM!"

She stumbled to her cot, where her divination board lay open, cowries scattered across it. She grabbed the board and brought it down across her knee. It broke cleanly into two halves, which she began to smash on the floor, over and over again, screaming with rage and pain and the niggling sense of betrayal. With each stroke a memory bloomed in her mind: Simbi venturing into the Inner Sanctum, emerging excited, asking her if she heard the voice, which orisha had chosen her.

(Smash!)

The countless hours she had spent hunched over the board, pondering the cowrie placements, hoping for a sign, anything.

(Smash!)

Being held here, like a bloody prisoner, all because she desired something that had come to everyone else with ease. But they had made a laughingstock of her, and she hated them. Hated every single one of them. Over and over again she smashed the board, until there was nothing left but splinters and she was kneeling there, panting, fists clenching and unclenching. Her hand was bleeding afresh, the stitches unravelled and the wound reopened. But she felt no pain; there was only anger. Bright, consuming anger. She wanted so badly to hurt someone, to make someone feel all the pain she felt, but she was all alone, save for the bird, which watched her through beady eyes.

"I'm done," she told it, sinking onto her cot. "I'm done with it all."

The bird took flight.

It gave a cry as it banked down the narrow passage, wings beating. Ashâke watched it go a moment, then took off after it. Perhaps there was a secret entrance she was unaware of. In her first days here, she had combed the place, searching for an alternate entrance, and had found none. But the bird had to have come from somewhere.

"Wait!" she cried. But the bird was swift, increasing the distance between them with each beat of its wings, and by the time Ashâke turned the corner, it had vanished. She stood there, panting, clutching the stitch in her side as she cast around for the kutu. She found herself at the end of the passage. The alcoves to her left and right were crammed with empty palm wine casks, as was the wall that marked the end of the passage, stacked floor to ceiling with casks. Old straw littered the rough floor, and dusty cobwebs stretched across the ceiling told her this place hadn't been used in a while. She made out some cracks in the ceiling, but none of them was large enough for a bird. So where did it go?

"Hello?" Ashâke called. "Where are you?"

Damn bird. It couldn't have simply vanished . . . unless . . . unless it had. Ashâke knew next to nothing about kutu, only that they were intelligent birds, smarter than ravens, and imprinted so hard on their owners that they often spoke in their voice.

A cold current of air kissed her legs. Ashâke dropped to her knees, eyes sweeping the walls and the floor, hands trailing through the straw. She felt it now on her face, a constant draught of cool air coming from—

There! There was a space between two barrels on the bottommost row, large enough for a bird to slip through. Heart beating in excitement, Ashâke crawled towards the barrels, ignoring the stabbing pain in her wounded hand. She squeezed an arm into the space and met empty air. She wiggled her hand about and met only more air. A slow grin spread over her face. This was it.

Moments later, she'd cleared the wall of casks, revealing a large, rectangular opening at the base of the wall. Ashâke dropped to her knees and crawled into it. She found herself on a tall bed of hay, and when she looked up, she realised why.

She was at the bottom of a chute that stretched up and into the darkness. This was where they pushed down casks of palm wine in harvest season to be stored, and the hay was no doubt to cushion the casks as they landed. Unused in a while, it was now overrun by rats, who chittered as they peered out of cracks in the walls of the chute.

She *was* done. She was leaving this blasted place, this blasted temple. Taking a deep breath, she stretched out her arms and began to shimmy up the chute.

By the time Ashâke reached the top grate, she was drenched in sweat, her arms and legs on fire from holding her up. Thankfully, the grate was open; she clambered out and collapsed to the floor, trying to catch her wind. She glimpsed a patch of star-spangled sky through the high kitchen window, and when she pushed to her feet, Ashâke realised she was in the kitchen. She began to mutter a prayer of thanks to the orisha that it was empty, but she caught herself. The orisha did not deserve her prayers. Not anymore.

She slipped out of the kitchen and down a corridor lit by torches guttering in their sconces. Their warm light washed across massive, colourful raffia mats that decorated the walls. A rite of accession, acolytes were made to weave decorative mats. Somewhere in the temple hung the mat she and Simbi had woven together, filled with scenes of bright birds and bright flowers of their future garden. They had made plans to buy a house together, to keep a garden bursting with fruits and birds. But that had been nearly five seasons ago, as they both prepared for accession, when Ashâke had been brimming with hope and possibility. Ashâke wondered if Simbi had purchased the birds. If she had purchased the house. If she was out there somewhere waiting for her.

I'm coming, Simbi, she thought. *I will find you.*

As she turned round the bend, she saw Priestess Essie leaving the Hall of Silence, a few acolytes scrambling in her wake like hatchlings after a hen. The priestess took one look at Ashâke and her eyes narrowed to slits.

"Stop right there, acolyte!"

Ashâke did not slow down, did not so much as acknowledge her.

"Acolyte! Just what do you think—?"

"Shut up!" Ashâke pushed past her.

The acolytes gasped, whispering amongst themselves. No doubt they had heard; they had all heard of her attempt to bind an orisha, of her incarceration in the larder. She wanted to claw at their faces, claw out those contemptuous eyes.

Priestess Essie's hand clamped around Ashâke's upper arm in a vise grip. "What?" She hissed, eyes bulging from her sockets in rage, her bosom heaving. "What did you say to me, *deaf priest*?"

Once, Ashâke would have fallen to her knees. Once, she would have grovelled and begged forgiveness, but that was what one who had a place in the temple would do, that was what one who bowed to Priestess Essie's authority and position as a priestess of Ifa would do. Ashâke was done grovelling. She was done taking shit from the orisha, much less from a priestess. She looked slowly and pointedly at Priestess Essie's hand, firmly clamped around her upper arm, and then up at the woman. "Unhand me, Priestess," she said quietly. "Before I make that hand forever useless."

Priestess Essie blinked. It was as though she could not fathom what was going on. She had apparently never been regarded with such open insubordination, and Ashâke could see the myriad emotions flitting across her features: confusion, rage, uncertainty. The priestess must have seen the look in Ashâke's eyes, however, must have gleaned the promise of violence, for she released her.

Ashâke snatched her arm away and stalked off.

"THE HIGH PRIESTESS WILL HEAR OF THIS!" the priestess cried after her. "I WILL HAVE YOU *OUT* OF THIS TEMPLE!"

I am already out of this temple. But there was no use wasting her breath on the woman. Ashâke moved quickly through the silent halls and out into the courtyard overlooking the forest beyond. On a night like this, a week or two ago, she had stolen across this very yard, terror and hope in her heart. Now she strolled across it and towards the gates with not a care in the world. Two paths forked away from the gates: the left one leading into the Sacred Grove with its cluster of white baobabs, the right one leading into the forest and the world beyond. Ashâke turned right.

She did not look back.

INTERLUDE II

Ba Fatai

The grass was cool under Ba Fatai's bare feet as he stepped into the glade. He wore only a loose piece of agbada, his pouch dangling at his hip. A ravine gurgled over moss-covered stones, black in the predawn light. On the other side of the ravine a fox drank, red tongue darting as it lapped up water. It raised its head at his approach, snout twitching, then loped off into the bushes. Ba Fatai stood a moment, looking at nothing in particular, then he reached behind his head and untied the cloth binding his Eye. Folding the cloth into a neat square, he tucked it into his pouch and lowered himself onto a boulder.

This was the place. This was where he would meet his end. He had had countless seasons to contemplate this moment, and yet, now that the time was come, he found that he was afraid. Ba Fatai supposed one could never really be prepared to die. He gave a dry chuckle. Everyone thought the White Eye a gift, when in truth it was a curse, when in truth they would never understand the burden it was to know the hour of your death.

Not that he had meant to know it. That was the first thing Olayaki taught him. "Never seek out the time or manner of your own death." But the Looking could hardly be controlled; it was at once like trying to dam a flood with a pebble while you slaked your thirst on its white waters—a double way to drown. And drown he had, the visions washing over him, overwhelming him, until he saw, very clearly, what was to come. He renounced his vows shortly after that, binding his Eye and locking away the future forever.

Or so he thought.

Now he reached into his pouch and took out his knife. Taking a deep breath, he pressed the knife into the flesh above his Eye, grunting as he worked it under the skin, cutting loose the charms that had held back his visions for forty seasons. Blood poured down his face, stinging his Eye, and he braced himself for the flood that was to come. Because it was there, he'd felt it, shivering in his bed for a thousand hellish nights as the visions sought to tear free. He almost stopped then, he almost replaced the nearly severed flap of skin.

But he had to know. He had to see.

Pain lanced through his Eye. Ba Fatai cried out, slipping off the boulder and falling to the ground. The Eye was hot, so hot he feared it was melting in its socket, burning a hole in his skull—

"Ngh!" he mewled, spittle flying from his lips. And there, in the black of dawn, the White Eye opened and the visions poured forth.

He saw a man seated upon a pile of bones, and on his face was a mask of gold, whose eye slits shone with the light of twin suns, so that none could behold him. He opened his hand

and out fell a raven that became two, that became three, that became thousands, dark wings flapping as they were loosed upon the world, borne upon the four winds to the corners of Aye. He opened the other hand and out fell a woman, and upon her skin was carved the thousand names of Olodumare, and she took her place at his right hand.

He saw the same woman, skin unblemished, riding a great winged elephant in a field of grass. The beast trumpeted, and the sound was echoed by another great winged elephant, who bore upon his back the Lord of Bones, who proclaimed in a voice of thunder: "I AM THE TEACHER, THE GREAT REDEMPTOR! I AM COME!"

And where they battled, man against woman, beast against beast, the world broke in two.

Ba Fatai came to, shuddering. His right cheek was pressed into the grass, and his Eye was sealed shut with crusted blood.

"Priest," said a voice. "You're a long way from your temple."

A boy was seated on the boulder, watching him. A scraggly child, dressed in clothes that were much too small for him. Ba Fatai might have taken him for an urchin, or a bandit, one who did not look strong enough to present any mortal danger.

Except for his eyes. Ba Fatai looked into them and did not find anything he recognised as human.

"I know who you are," groaned Fatai.

The boy smiled. "Good. Very good. I would say I have

no quarrel with you, but that would be a lie. Still, I am not unkind. You will lead me back to your temple, and I will show you the Teacher's mercy."

"I will do no such thing."

"It would cost nothing to take possession of your body, and your memories, and find the temple myself. Which will it be?"

They remained unmoving for a moment, the boy watching Ba Fatai with a lazy smirk. Ba Fatai's eyes slid to his knife, glinting in the grass where it had fallen when the vision took him. The boy traced his gaze and smiled even wider.

At that moment there came a bloodcurdling screech as a bird burst out of the trees. Ba Fatai turned to see a streak of red and orange blow past him and crash into the boy in an explosion of feathers. His kutu. He had bid the bird remain in the temple, yet here it was, helping him. Ba Fatai had never been more grateful for its disobedience.

The boy fell to the ground, crying out as he tried to shield his eyes from the kutu's slashing claws. He flailed, kicking, managed to seize the bird by its neck. A twist, and a sharp crack, and the bird hung limp from his hand.

"NO!" cried Ba Fatai.

The boy flung the bird's lifeless body into the ravine and sat up. Both eyes were ruined, their jellies running down his cheek; still, he turned in Ba Fatai's direction as though he could see. A moment passed, in which the ravine gurgled over the rocks, in which a bird shrieked in the distance, and then he dropped to the ground like a puppet whose strings had been cut, unmoving.

Ba Fatai sat there, panting, staring at the boy. Was he dead? Had his kutu somehow managed to strike a killing blow? Then a cloud of purple-black smoke seeped out of the body, and before Ba Fatai could comprehend what he was seeing, it rushed towards him and enveloped him.

With a guttural croak, Ba Fatai began to convulse, kicking and frothing at the mouth. He felt a foreign presence squeeze itself into his body, into his mind, and though he fought with everything he had, he was no match for it. He was slowly being consumed.

All those seasons ago when he saw himself take his life, he had been baffled, wondering what would drive him to do such a thing. But now he understood. He understood everything. His life, for the protection of those that remained.

Ba Fatai's hands closed around the leather handle of the knife and he drove it into his heart.

FIVE

It was midmorning, and by the slant of sunlight through the leaves, Ashâke fathomed it was about three hours after dawn. She had walked some distance the previous night, driven by anger and the burning need to put as much space as possible between herself and the temple. So she'd walked farther into the forest than she ever had, until she could no longer see the looming mountain temple, or the numerous lantern lights that lit it up, until, exhausted, she had clambered into the bough of a dead tree and drifted off into fitful sleep.

Now she sat in the tree, staring at nothing in particular. Her body told her she should go to the Hall of Silence for morning prayers, but there would be no more morning prayers for her. Not now, not anymore.

An immense sadness washed over her. Part of her had hoped it had all been a dream, some terrible vision conjured up by her mind. But it wasn't, and in the stark light of day, the reality of it hit her hard: she had left the only home she'd ever known. The orisha had no use for her, and she in turn renounced them. It was a frightening prospect, a worrying one, to find herself so suddenly untethered, but she was set in her decision. For the first time ever, she was in control of her life.

"I am free," she said to no one in particular. Then, louder: "I AM FREE!"

Ashâke stared at the identical trees, coming to the slow realisation that she hadn't really given this much thought. She did not know how to find her way out of the forest. Now that she thought of it, the farther from the temple she ventured, the more likely it was that she would get lost. Would she roam the forests indefinitely, forced to fend for herself, depending on wild mushrooms and game, so starved of human contact that she became a thing of the wild, indistinguishable from the animals that kept her company?

Bloody priests. This was all their fault. Although they went and came as they pleased, acolytes were forbidden from wandering the forest, from even leaving the temple unaccompanied. Now here she was, without the slightest clue where to go. Oh, she knew of the surrounding cities: Inysha and Oyo and even Offa, where sweet potatoes grew in abundance. It was getting there, finding any one of them—that was another matter.

No. Now was not the time to despair. She took the sun's location and set off in the opposite direction. The forest did not go on forever, and if she kept heading west, sooner or later she was bound to come out of it. She tried not to think when that would be.

The sun was already high in the sky, her clothes sticking to her sweaty back, when Ashâke heard the sound. At first, she thought it some hallucination, conjured by heat and hunger, but then she saw the glint of silver through the trees, a vast expanse of rippling water reflecting the white sky, and she knew that this was no hallucination. She'd found a river.

"Haha!" she cried, as she broke out of the trees and onto its muddy banks. "Yes! Yes! YES!" She waded into the shallows and dropped to her knees, the water seeping into her clothes and cooling her ass. She cupped her hands, scooped up water, and brought it to her lips. It was cool and sweet as it travelled down her throat. Obatala's breath, water had never felt so good! When she could not scoop fast enough to slake her thirst she drank straight from the river, gulping it up like a beast at a watering hole. Once satisfied, she splashed farther into the river until the sand vanished beneath her feet and she gave herself up to the water. Floating on her back, she watched the white sky and its wispy clouds as the slow currents ferried her farther from the banks. She would follow the river. Eventually it would lead to a settlement. And from there she could find her way to Inysha and maybe find Simbi—

Voices.

Ashâke froze, her heart thrashing in her chest. She flipped over, eyes frantically searching the trees for the source of the voices. Then she abandoned all caution and splashed for the banks, a dozen thoughts racing through her mind. What had she been thinking, exposing herself like this? Stupid, stupid, *stupid*. Grisly tales of brigands skulking in the wild and accosting unsuspecting travellers came to her. And she was a woman, alone in the forest.

She stumbled out of the water, gasping and sopping wet, then raced for the trees. Twice she tripped, nearly planting face-first in the mud, but at the last moment she regained her balance and continued on. Once in the safety of the forest, she clambered up a tree, pain darting through the wound in her hand, skinning her knees and arms on the hard bark. Finally, she swung onto a huge branch and pressed herself flat against it like a leopard. Then she waited. It was no use running without knowing from which direction they were coming.

Through the chaos of trees and leaves she made out the river, gilded in the late afternoon sun—

"Shit!" she hissed. Her footprints were pressed into the soft riverbank, leading up to the trees. She might as well have drawn a big arrow pointing in her direction.

The wind carried the voices downriver, and the more she listened, the more it sounded like there was quite a number of them. Had she reached a settlement?

A scream rent the air. High and bloodcurdling, it sent a few squirrels scampering for safety. Ashâke hugged the branch tighter, heart thudding in her chest, wondering who the scream belonged to, if the brigands had found their quarry.

And then she saw them.

Two children came tearing down the bank, kicking up sand and screaming at the top of their lungs as they fled.

Behind them, fast closing the gap, was a grown man, his face hidden behind a mask.

Without thought, Ashâke slid down the tree, slipping her knife from its pouch. She landed in a sprawl, nearly impaling herself on her knife, but sprang to her feet and raced for the children. She had never fought in her life, had never so much as pulled her taunting juniors by the hair, no matter how deserving of it they had been. Yet here she was, racing to face a stranger, one who was nearly twice her size. Some small, self-preserving part of her screamed at her to stop, to turn back while she still had the chance, but she kept on running.

A child stumbled, fell. The other paused to help, but they had slowed down long enough for the man to close the distance.

In three bounding strides he reached them, pounced, and they crashed into the sand in a tangle of limbs and—

Laughter. They were *laughing*. What Ashâke had taken for screams of fear and panic were actually squeals of delight. She staggered to a halt, panting, gawking with a mixture of confusion and wonder as they tussled in the sand. The man had managed to untangle himself. Now he gave a great roar and pinned both children down with his large hands, which he began to burrow into their bellies as he tickled them.

Screams of joy filled the air, interspersed with breathless laughter as they tried to squirm away from his tickling hands.

Even as Ashâke watched, another child came tearing down the bank, moving as swift as the wind. With a shriek of delight, she leapt at the man, latching onto his back. Then she reached around and yanked free his mask to reveal the laughing face of a young man, long plaits flying about.

"Jagu no-face!" she cried triumphantly, holding the mask aloft. The man roared and the children squealed with delight. The two children squirming in the sand twisted free just as the girl leapt off his back.

"Jagu no-face! Jagu no-face!" they cried.

"Ay! Ay!" said the man as they swarmed him. "Fine, I give up! Oh, you're too strong! How can I ever stand against you?"

And then he was on the flat of his back and they were dancing around him, tossing the mask between themselves as they chanted, "Jagu no-face! Jagu no-face!"

Ashâke found that she was smiling, marvelling at the pure joy on their faces, like they had not a care in the world. It was a beautiful sight. She couldn't remember a time *she* had laughed with such abandon, not even as a child.

"My turn to be Jagu," said the girl, the one who had unmasked the man.

"Where did you hide?" asked one of the boys.

"Yes. Where?" chimed the other.

Ashâke looked from one boy to the next. They were twins! From the crown of their heads to the clothes they wore, they were identical copies of each other. Twins were good luck, that much she knew. She started to think how blessed their mother was, to have the favour of Ibeji, patron orisha of twins, but stopped herself. Gone were the days when she prayed to the orisha, when she saw their meaning and intent in every happening. No. She did not care a hoot for them. Fuck them.

"In the forest," said the girl excitedly. She looked to be older than the twins, though not by much. And the man, was he their brother? "I ran into the forest."

"What?" The man looked genuinely alarmed. He wagged a finger at her as she danced out of his reach. "Ay, Ralia, you little fox. You shouldn't go into the forest. Your mother would kill me if I lost you."

Their father, then? But he looked too young to be their father. He looked to be roughly Ashâke's age.

The girl stuck out her tongue.

"I should pluck out your tongue and eat it," said the man. "No. We won't go again until you promise not to go running in the forest."

"But that's no fun!"

"What's no fun is your father making a drum of my skin if I lost you."

"You'll make a very big drum."

"Yes. I know. Thank you. Now, promise you won't go in the forest."

Ralia pouted, but it was only for show. She touched a finger to her tongue, then her forehead, then pointed at the sky. "Promise." The twins did the same. Ashâke grinned, remembering all the times she had made Simbi swear in a similar manner.

"Then we are agreed!" the man said, grinning. "Let us—"

A sharp crack as a twig snapped beneath Ashâke's feet.

She froze, a rabbit in a trap, as they whipped in her direction. She didn't even know it but she had been inching towards them. Wanting to be closer to them or to see them better? She couldn't say. Now four pairs of eyes were turned in her direction.

"What is it?" asked the first twin.

"Maybe an animal," said the man, frowning as he slowly rose to his feet. Ashâke had never been more grateful as she was in that moment for the dark forest and the close-growing trees. "See why I told you not to go in the forest? There are wild animals there that'll rip you limb from limb."

"I'm not scared, Uncle Djola," said Ralia, and he sighed, throwing up his hands. Ashâke had the feeling this was an old argument.

"Do you think it is Jagu?" asked one of the boys in a hushed whisper. "The *real* Jagu?"

"Let us hope it is not. Come, we must return to camp. Your mothers will be wondering where you are."

Camp. There was a camp nearby. That would explain the voices she had heard. Ashâke wondered just how large the camp was, and how many people were there.

They were already walking away, so Ashâke followed them. She kept to the forest, moving lightly. The children kept up a constant chatter all the way, never walking quietly but dancing around Djola, who suffered them. Ashâke was just beginning to wonder how much farther their camp was when they turned the corner.

"Stars above."

Eight huge boats idled in the river. Each vessel was onion-shaped, their hulls covered with brightly painted whorl patterns: purple and orange and sky blue. There were other smaller boats—Ashâke counted at least two dozen—tethered one to the other with thick ropes so as not to drift away. It looked like a floating city. It *was* a floating city. It looked like people could live their whole lives—get married, have children, die—on these boats.

"Griots," Ashâke breathed. She felt her skin tingling with excitement. The shape of those boats, those patterns. She had seen them in library books, and would have recognised them anywhere. These people were griots. All her life she had heard of these nomads, who were called the world's memory: they spun long-forgotten events into songs, recalling every arcane bit of history all the way to the creation of Aye. The priests argued that they were frauds, that it was impossible for the human mind to remember everything or to hold that much knowledge. What was it they said? *Beware the griots. They will embellish for the sake of rhyme, warp to keep in time.* Still, others said they were gifted with long memory. The ashe that ran through their blood allowed it. Standing here, Ashâke could not help but feel like they were right.

She edged closer, dangerously close to the forest's edge, the better to see.

There were so many children. They splashed in the water, their shrieks filling the air as they frolicked and worked the river into a lather. On shore, people milled about, consumed with one task or the other: several men laboured at one boat, some lugging freshly chopped wood, others hauling buckets of bubbling resin as they worked to patch up a breach in the hull; some women squatted halfway in the shallows, washing dirty laundry, occasionally yelling at the disruptive children who splashed up waves that threatened to suck the clothes away; others were gathered about several cookfires, sweating over humongous pots.

It was, truly, an encampment.

Dusk had fallen and brought with it a chill. Mist clung to the surface of the river and made ghost vessels of the boats. The griots were gathered about several fires, attending their dinner. The soft chatter of conversation and occasional raucous laughter, not to mention the mouth-watering aroma of yam porridge, wafted down towards Ashâke. She was hungry. She had gone nearly a day without food, and while she wished she could join them, she wasn't sure about confronting three hundred strangers. So she crouched in the trees some two hundred strides from the camp, not daring to go any closer for fear that someone seeking the outhouse would wander her way and stumble upon her.

"You should come join us," said a voice behind her.

Ashâke leapt to her feet, whipped around.

Djola stood before her, leaning casually against a tree. He had washed the mud from his hair and had changed into a coal-grey buba and shokoto overlaid with a breastplate of hard-boiled leather, all of which blended with his dark skin. He was almost one with the dark, which she thought was his intent. Ashâke made him out only by the flicker of firelight that cut through the trees, and not by much. He looked much bigger up close, and Ashâke was all too aware the ease with which he could overpower her if he wanted. She was even more disturbed by the fact that he had snuck up on her and she'd been completely oblivious.

He took a step towards her.

Ashâke reacted without thinking, whipping out her knife. It flew from her hand with the force of the movement, bounced off the nearest tree and sank sadly to the ground. Cursing, she fished for it through the damp undergrowth, found it, then resumed her position three strides from Djola, pointing her knife at him.

"Do you mean to stick me with that?" he said. "What a threatening sight you make."

"Good. Then you know—" She broke off, frowning. It occurred to her that he hadn't moved at all through her display, had simply stood there, watching her, an inscrutable expression on his face. Matter of fact, she had never seen anyone look less threatened. "You mock me."

Djola grinned, flashing white teeth. "I wouldn't dare. Although I should point out that the knife you so masterfully wield is a bread knife. Good for cutting . . . bread." He reached into his belt and with a flourish produced a wicked-looking dagger. It glinted in the dark as he admired the edge. "This here's a boning knife. Sharp enough to wound, why, even kill a man—if you know where to hit. This is what you want, if you mean to attack me."

Why would he tell her that? Was he trying to intimidate her? Yes, that knife did look sharp. Painfully so. And Ashâke did not want to imagine the many ways he could gut her. So she pushed the thoughts from her mind and waved her knife in his face. "A knife is a knife. And I know where to cut you to make you hurt. So stay back."

Djola grinned even wider, then made a show of returning his dagger to his belt. "My apologies. I did not mean to frighten you—"

"I'm not frightened—"

"—but in all fairness, you brought out your knife first. One should not wave a knife about if one does not mean to use it."

They stood there a long while, eyeing each other. Ashâke's hand was starting to ache, and she realised she looked ridiculous pointing a bread knife at him. Still, she wasn't about to let down her guard. He was a stranger, no matter how disarming he seemed. He still had that boning knife, and she was alone with him in the forest, far enough away from the camp that they wouldn't hear her cry . . .

"Where did you come from?" she asked. "Why aren't you with your people? How did you know I was here?"

"So many questions," he said, slowly crossing his arms. Ashâke could not help but notice the way his muscles bulged. "I saw you watching us downriver."

She cursed inwardly. Of course he had seen her. She thought she had been well hidden in the trees; apparently not. Ashâke was starting to learn that she was not very good at being . . . a runaway? A wild woman?

"So you followed me."

"In a manner of speaking. I came back to find you."

Ashâke swallowed. "Came back to find me. Why?"

"To make sure you did not present a danger to me and my people." He said it lightly enough, but there was no denying the undercurrent of menace.

Was he some kind of watchman? That made sense. The forests were dangerous, and there would be watchmen in a camp this large. A camp filled with so many women and children. Djola must have decided she was no danger, otherwise they wouldn't be speaking so calmly. Then again, there could be others lurking in the shadows. Watchmen like him.

"My friends are coming," she said. "They went hunting."

"Of course." His tone made it clear that he knew she

was lying. If he was the watchman she suspected him to be, he would have made sure she was alone before showing himself.

"What do you want?"

"Ah." Djola tapped his jaw thoughtfully. "Now *that* is a question for you. What do you want? What are you doing out here . . . without your friends?"

Running. Running from the temple and a failed life of service. Running from the orisha, who'd rejected her. Not that one could ever really run from the orisha. "It's no business of yours."

His eyes lingered on her wounded hand, on the filthy, bloodstained bandage. "Maybe so. But it's not often we come across acolytes lost in the wild."

"How did you . . . ?" She trailed off. She was still in her priestly raiment, shabby as it was. Ashâke didn't know which stung more, that he took her immediately for an acolyte, or that he did not even stop to consider that she was actually a priest. A woman her age should be a priest. She felt an all too familiar rage bubble up, but she clamped down on it.

He smirked. "You look hungry. Cold. We have plenty of food and a warm fire. And a pallet where you can sleep. I don't know what you've heard about my people, but we're generally harmless." He considered. "Except for Ralia, you should stay away from her. That little girl is a menace."

A smile tugged at Ashâke's lips. Ralia *had* looked too

much for him to handle. What she needed was an older sister, one who'd . . . stars above, what was she thinking? That *she'd* be the older sister? She looked towards the camp. The fires did look warm and inviting. And she *was* starving. But she was also wary. All her life she'd known the same people. The prospect of so many strangers frightened her. Not to mention, how would she explain how she came to be here? How would she explain the cut in her hand?

"No," she said. "My friends . . . will be worried. Thank you, though."

Djola stared at her and then slowly nodded. "As you wish." He paused a moment. "I'll be watching for your friends."

And he stalked off into the night.

SIX

"Praise be. You're alive."

A woman stood over Ashâke. She wore iro and buba of muted colours, with bright whorl patterns—the same ones on the boats—spattered across them in beautiful contrast. Several loops of coral beads and shells adorned her neck, bouncing against her ample bosom as she leaned over Ashâke. Her grey-silver hair was pulled into four stern plaits, braided with cowries. She looked old enough to have seen sixty or seventy rain seasons. She peered down at Ashâke through kohl-lined eyes, worry etched across her features.

Ashâke blinked, trying to drag her mind from the murky depths of sleep.

She remembered watching the camp until the fires burned low and the griots began to retire, calling to one another as they stumbled for their tents or boats. She remembered retracing her steps, before finally finding a patch of dry ground at the base of a tree where she nestled and settled into sleep. She thought she had chosen a secluded spot, a place where she wouldn't be so easily found. Apparently not. It had to be Djola, of course. He had tracked her easily enough last night.

Ashâke sat up. Her bones were stiff from sleeping on the hard ground, and her clothes stuck to her, wet with dew. Behind her the faint noise of the camp filled the morning air: men yelling, mothers calling for their children, children shrieking as they played.

"Of course she's alive," said Djola as he stepped into view. "Why wouldn't she be?"

"Why wouldn't . . ." The woman closed her eyes and rounded on him. "Tonight I will have you sleep out here, with nothing but the clothes on your back."

Djola shrugged. "I can survive a little cold—"

"Shut up, boy. Don't make me smack you." She turned back to Ashâke. "Can you walk?"

"Can I . . . ?" Of course she could walk, why wouldn't she be able to?

"Good, you're coming with me." With surprising strength, she pulled Ashâke to her feet, who cried out as pain spasmed through her wound.

"What is—ah . . . you're injured." She glared at Djola. "I can't believe you left her out here."

"Aunty, as I said, I invited her. She refused. I couldn't well *force* her—"

"Why not? Look at the poor child! Does she seem fine to you?"

"Well—"

"So very tactless. But you got that from your father."

Djola opened his mouth to protest, but the woman had already dismissed him. "Come, daughter. Come with me at once." And before Ashâke could so much as open her mouth, the woman linked arms with her and steered her towards the camp.

After the gloom of the forest, the sunlight was harsh on Ashâke's eyes, so that she was forced to squint, cantering after the woman like a mule. She felt like she'd been shoved off a cliff without warning. She wanted to scream, or at least ask for a chance to catch up, but everything was happening so fast, and she found herself strangely flustered, as though she were merely an observer to what was happening.

"What is your name, child?"

"Ashâke."

"You can call me Mama Agba. That dolt Djola is my nephew, my sister's boy. Although you wouldn't know that. How tactless he can be sometimes."

Ashâke cast over her shoulder, where Djola was bringing up the rear, his face flitting between embarrassment and exasperation. He saw her looking and glowered at her. "It's not his fault, really. I told him I was fine."

"Mm-hmm."

Ashâke got the idea the woman typically only heard what she wanted to, and no one could change her mind. She reminded Ashâke of Ba Fatai. But this was the last thing she expected, a concerned woman steering her to warmth and safety. But then again, only the previous night Djola himself had invited her to join them. Could these people really be so . . . open towards strangers?

Ashâke was mildly alarmed to find that they were collecting quite the entourage. Children swarmed her: Ralia and the twins, tall children, gangly children, snot-nosed brats, all of them gawking openly at her with childish curiosity.

"Who's your friend?" she heard Ralia ask, to which Djola replied, "She's not my friend."

Ashâke wished the ground would open up and swallow her. This was precisely what she had been trying to avoid, this unwanted attention. She felt as though she was back in the temple, in a divination class, stuttering over the board while Priest Fawole tutted at her shoulder, telling her to apply herself, to open her mind. Now everyone's eyes were on her, a hundred strangers' eyes appraising her, judging her. What would they make of her? She knew what a sight she made, with leaves in her hair and mud on her clothes. She looked like one of the brigands she so acutely feared.

They passed by a boat, one of the three larger ones, whose broken hull the men were repairing. Ashâke kept her gaze on the ground, feeling their eyes like pinpricks on her.

"Nothing to see," Mama Agba said to the children. "Go away, or I'll find some work for you. All of you."

And then they were on a boat. Ashâke had never been on a boat and she found the sudden change overwhelming. The mere thought that beneath her was not solid ground but water turned her stomach to mush, and she was more than grateful in that instant that her stomach was empty, or she would have certainly emptied it. Mama Agba led her belowdecks where she slid open a wooden door and ushered Ashâke into the room beyond.

It was a small, comfy room, filled with all the trappings of a lifetime of possessions. Blue tie-dye curtains fluttered over a window that looked out to the river, and just beneath it stood a massive chest overflowing with clothes. Pushed up into the corner was a wooden tub and bucket, still wet from an earlier bath. A sleeping mat was spread in the centre of the room, more clothes strewn across it.

"Ok, we must wash you," said Mama Agba. "Are you hungry? You must be hungry."

"I . . . yes, ma . . ." An ancient silver-framed mirror skulked in the corner. Ashâke caught her flustered expression in the cracked glass.

"I will find you something to eat while you wash." Mama Agba fetched the bucket and thrust it out the window. "I see you, Ralia," she said. "Go fetch water for a bath, since you have nothing better to do. *Ralia!*"

A small hand appeared at the window, snatched the bucket, and vanished.

Ashâke stood there, wringing her hands. She did not know what she had expected, but certainly not this woman who, not knowing her, had embraced her wholeheartedly. Called her "daughter." It was all too much. It was more kindness than she had experienced in all her life.

She burst into tears. Racking, heaving tears.

"Oh," said Mama Agba, her eyes going round. "Oh, child . . ."

Ashâke turned away, embarrassed, rubbing at her eyes. But she felt Mama Agba's arms around her, and all the fight bled from her. She wept into her bosom, allowing herself to be cuddled, allowing herself to be petted. All she'd ever wanted was to feel like she belonged. And here, on this boat, in this camp filled with griots, in this room in the embrace of the matriarch, she was starting to feel at home in a way she never had at the temple.

The door opened and Ralia came in bearing a bucket of water. She frowned at them as she emptied the bucket into the tub.

"Why are you crying? Are you hurt?"

"Ralia, I swear—" the matriarch began.

"No, it's alright," said Ashâke. She gave the girl a watery smile. "I was hurt, but I'm . . . healing."

Ralia studied Ashâke through large, curious eyes, then seemed to arrive at a conclusion. "Good."

"Alright, come along," said Mama Agba, rising to her feet. She offered her hand and Ralia took it. "Let us leave our new friend to her bath." To Ashâke, she added, "Knock on the door when you are finished and I will come."

Soon Ashâke was washed, dressed in fresh clothes that were a little too big for her, and treated to a mouth-watering breakfast of ogi and akara. Ravenous though she had been, Ashâke found that she now did not have much of an appetite, and after poking at her food and forcing down a few more spoonfuls under Mama Agba's watchful eye, she pushed aside the remnants of her breakfast with an apologetic grimace, promising to attend to it before the morning was spent.

She sat on the pallet in Mama Agba's room, the stench of poultice thick in the air as the woman dressed her wound.

"You have not asked how I came about this wound," she said. There were many things the woman had not asked, like where she came from, although it was not hard to guess that she was an acolyte. Perhaps she thought her fleeing the temple. And she wouldn't be wrong. Perhaps Ashâke was not the first fleeing acolyte she'd met.

"Do you want me to?" She dabbed the wound, causing Ashâke to inhale sharply. "A young woman alone in the wild—there are many, many ways to get injured."

"And you're not curious . . . you don't wish to know *why* I'm here?"

Mama Agba smiled. "Child. Half the people in this camp have come to us in some manner or the other. Some were babies abandoned by their parents. Either because they had one too many mouths to feed already, or believed the word of some hack shaman who pronounced them cursed. Others were cast from their families, cast from society, shunned and ostracised. And since we do not belong to any one kingdom, since we live, in a manner of speaking, at the edge of society, we take them in. It doesn't matter where you come from, if you are in need, there's always a place for you among us."

Ashâke imagined the tribe as one giant rake, ploughing through the Ten Kingdoms and picking up strays. And perhaps, too, collecting gems.

"I cut my hand in a binding ritual." She gave a dry, bitter laugh. "I tried to summon an orisha, which was foolish of me, but . . . I suppose it doesn't matter anymore. The orisha do not want me."

A curious look crossed Mama Agba's features, but it was there so briefly Ashâke fathomed she had imagined it.

"There," said the matriarch as she looped the bandage and tied it up. "Now try to be careful with that hand, so you don't reopen the wound."

Ralia found Ashâke once she stepped off the boat.

"Do you want to play Jagu-Jagu?"

"What?"

She frowned up at her. "Haven't you played Jagu-Jagu before?"

No. No, she hadn't. Not Jagu-Jagu or any other games. Her childhood had been given to an ascetic life of prayer and deep contemplation. Ralia seemed positively scandalised by the idea that she hadn't played the game and insisted on rectifying the situation. So Ashâke found herself wearing a mask, chasing after the children who scattered before her, squealing as they tripped over themselves in an effort to get away from her. Ashâke found herself laughing, chanting, "Jagu no-face, Jagu no-face."

"What are you doing?" asked Ralia as they prepared to go another round.

"What?"

"You keep looking at the trees. Are you . . . ?" Her eyes went round as she leaned in conspiratorially. "Are there more of you coming?"

"More of . . . me?"

"Priests!" she hissed impatiently, as though Ashâke were the child, and a slow one at that.

"No." She hoped there weren't. She wanted to get as far away from the priests as possible.

In the afternoon, after the children had been forced into siesta, Ashâke joined the women at the river, offering to wash some clothes, but they refused her when they saw her bandaged hand, shooing her away good-naturedly. Ashâke wandered the camp until she came across a grizzled old man stringing a kora. His deep brown skin was lined, and what little hair he had left was sprinkled across his scalp like salt. He smiled at her and asked if she would like a song. When she began to decline—she didn't want to trouble him, after all—he waved away her protests and insisted she sit while he finished stringing the instrument. He talked as he worked. He told her there were three large families in the tribe, although amongst them the concept of strict filial ties was almost moot, so that one child would as soon suckle from his mother's breast as suckle at the breast of a woman from the next boat. Indeed, each person cared for the other as though they were related by blood. She learned that the tribe as a whole was headed by Baale Jaha, Mama Agba's husband, who had been patriarch and Master Griot for near fifty seasons and could recite events as far back as the Creation, when Obatala descended from Orun and cast a bowlful of sand into the sea to form land. The tribe had been travelling from Skaggás when they ran into a rapids, destroying the hull of the second boat. Their next port of call was Inysha, and Ashâke hoped they would allow her to go with them. She would love to see the city, and maybe, hopefully, see Simbi.

Ashâke caught glimpses of Mama Agba, always flitting from one place to the next, and Ashâke understood how lucky she had been to have had her attention for even a short while.

Dinner was an elaborate affair. The tribe gathered about several fire pits to eat a meal of flatbread and pepper soup filled with chunky helpings of boiled mushrooms and fish, sprinkled with bitter leaves and roast onions. It was delicious, and Ashâke filled herself to bursting, her appetite returned. She was seated with the main group, with Baale Jaha and Mama Agba and several other people whose acquaintance she had made over the course of the day. Ralia sat next to her, and once they had eaten their fill, the girl curled up against Ashâke, her hair smelling faintly of coconut oil.

A young woman went about with a big pot, ladling second helpings into the bowls of those who wished.

"I'll have some more!" roared a big, bearded man Ashâke had come to know as Gaza, Ralia's father and one of the main drummers of the group.

"No, you won't," said his wife, snatching his proffered bowl from him. "I don't want to have to suffer your farts at night because you've glutted yourself."

Laughter rippled through the camp as he spluttered in indignation. Ashâke found herself laughing too. Perhaps it was the wine, perhaps it was simply the good company, but in that moment she forgot her woes, that she had left the temple, that the orisha had no use for her. To think that only yesterday she had been skulking in the bushes, looking on from the outside and wishing to be among their number. Now here she was, sitting and laughing with them as though they had known each other for many seasons. Ba Fatai had been right after all, her future was not in the temple. Her future was out here, in the world, among the griots and the camaraderie they offered.

"Where are you going?" Ralia asked as Ashâke rose to her feet.

"Need to empty my bladder."

"Oh . . . don't let Jagu catch you," she whispered, eyes twinkling in the firelight, and Ashâke grinned.

Far from the warmth of the fires, the evening had taken on a chill, and dew-wet underbrush raked her ankles as Ashâke walked into the woods. The mating call of a frog, perhaps several frogs, filled the air. She soon found a clearing, filled with waist-length elephant grass. Bunching up her clothes about her waist, she squatted and let go.

The grass moved. At first Ashâke thought it was an animal scurrying away at the sound of her stream, then she saw the boy watching her through the grass.

"What are you doing?" she cried, springing to her feet as she hastily yanked up her undergarment and pulled down her clothes. "Were you *watching* me?"

The boy made no effort to bolt, or even hide his face. He simply stood, staring at her. His gaze was intense, hungry. It did not belong on the face of a boy of twelve seasons, and it unnerved her.

"What is your name?" Her crotch still burned from a piss that was cut short.

"You came from the temple, didn't you?" he asked. "There must be a temple around here. Do you know where it is?"

Ashâke frowned. The various locations of the temples were a closely guarded secret, with pathways to and fro known only to priests.

"Why do you ask?"

"I want to go there," he said.

"You can't. Only priests and acolytes are allowed there."

He cocked his head, considering. "You are a priest. You can take me."

"No. I'm not going back." She paused. "Do you *want* to be a priest?" That would explain his interest, but he was a little too old for initiation, not to mention he was already—

He moved fast. One moment he stood some five strides from her, hidden in the elephant grass, the next he was before her, standing in her piss, hand clamped tight around her wrist.

"Aaah," she cried. "What is wrong with you—let me—!"

"What's going on here?"

Djola stepped into the clearing, machete on his shoulder, a frown on his face. He looked from Ashâke to the boy, who let go of her immediately. "Nothing. Me and the priest were just having a talk, that's all."

"You were peeping on me!" Ashâke cried, rubbing the spot where he'd grabbed her. Obatala's breath, his grip was iron. She never would have imagined such strength from such a wisp of a boy.

"That so?" Djola turned his frown on the boy. "Were you watching the woman in her private moment?"

A mumble.

"Speak up, boy!"

"Wasn't peeping. Was waiting for her. Wanted to talk."

Djola cuffed him. Hard. The boy yelped and jumped backwards, clutching his ear.

"Off with you," said Djola.

He gave them both baleful stares, then stalked away like a chastised cat.

"You didn't have to do that," said Ashâke.

Djola raised his eyebrows. "You're the one who said he was watching you."

"Yes, but . . ." She bit her lip. "You could have simply scolded him."

"Eh." Djola shrugged. "When next he thinks to peep on a woman, he'll remember my hand. Sometimes a hard hand is better than words." He frowned. "Strange lad. I don't know how he thinks it's okay to watch people. What, did I say something funny?"

Ashâke was smiling. "No, it's just . . . isn't that what you do too? Peep?"

It took Djola a moment to digest what she'd said. "What? That is different!"

"Is it? You did sneak up on me yesterday, and now, did you just happen to stroll past where I came to pass water?"

Djola blinked. "You can't be—do you accuse me of—I was on patrol! Listen, I would never—"

Ashâke burst out laughing. "I jest! Gods, I only jest!" She dabbed at her eyes. "Oh, you should see your face, you look constipated."

Djola wore an expression of genuine bafflement. "What kind of a woman are you?"

He spun on his feet and stormed off towards camp, Ashâke hurrying after him, still laughing, calling out that she had only been jesting.

SEVEN

"Are you going to stay with us?" Ralia asked as Ashâke resumed her place beside her at the fire.

"Ralia. That is her decision to make," said Mama Agba, bouncing a fussing babe on her thighs. "And she will tell us when she's ready, so stop hounding her."

"But you won't go back, will you? To the temple."

"No. I do not plan to return," said Ashâke.

Ralia smiled, and Ashâke was touched to see the relief in that smile. Had the girl really taken to her that quickly? "Good," she said, snuggling closer to Ashâke. Then, "There are no orisha, so you shouldn't—"

"Ralia!" hissed Mama Agba, eyes shooting daggers at the girl.

Ashâke felt her mouth go suddenly dry. "What?" She looked up at them. "What is she talking about?"

Mama Agba sighed. "I thought you knew, I thought perhaps that was why you . . . left, but then you said in my room, 'the orisha do not want me.' Child. The orisha have no want because they are dead."

Silence fell over the camp, broken only by the crackle of logs in the fire. Somewhere an animal called. Ashâke realised that they were all looking at her.

"That is not true," she chuckled weakly. "It can't be."

"Do you hear them?" It was Baale Jaha who spoke, his deep voice rumbling in her chest. "The priests of old used to be able to speak to the orisha. Hear their voices in their heads all the time."

"I can't hear them because I'm not a priest," Ashâke explained. "It's only after we accede that we—you see, there's a ceremony where the orisha *choose* and they never chose me . . ."

It sounded a bit hollow, all of a sudden. The reasoning. They clung to the faith that all they were taught was true. *She* had clung to the faith that she would one day hear the orisha. But faith was so easily manipulated. After all, what was faith but belief in something intangible? Something unseen, something *unheard*. And hadn't she believed all these seasons? Their service hinged on communion with the orisha. But *if* the orisha were dead, how could the priests claim to commune with them? How could they claim to hear them?

The answer came to her, stark in its truth. *They're lying. They're all pretending.*

She wanted to believe. It would explain a lot. It would explain why, try as hard as she might, she had never been able to hear them. Had everyone simply gone into the Inner Sanctum and come out pretending to have been chosen? Pretending to be able to hear the orisha? Ashâke felt like the brunt of a terrible jape, a jape to which everyone but her had been privy. But why? Why would the priests lie? Why would Simbi lie to her?

"The orisha . . . are not dead. They can't be . . ." Now it was a plea. A desperate, useless plea. Because the truth would mean she was a fool. Had been a fool all her life. But the truth was clear. Now that it had been pointed out, it seemed so obvious. Hadn't she suspected that the priests had been lying to her? Hadn't she wondered that they had been keeping the truth from her? This was the true reason they forbade acolytes from leaving the temple. So they wouldn't learn the truth. This was why they had panicked when she tried and failed to summon an orisha.

Comprehension dawned on her: there had been no orisha to summon because they were all dead.

Something hot ran down her cheeks. Ashâke touched two fingers to her face and stared in confusion when they came away glistening with tears. Slowly, she began to laugh. Mirthless, joyless laughter bubbled up her belly, up her throat, until she doubled over, smacking her thighs and shuddering with gales of it. What a strange sight she made in that camp, her laughter echoing like a hyena's call through the chill night, washing over the river and the trees and the mountains. And when she looked at the griots, saw the worry and pity and concern replicated on their faces, she only laughed more, laughed harder, because she *was* a fool. She laughed until it hurt even to breathe, until she spent herself and could laugh no more. And then she said into the silence, "How?"

Mama Agba glanced at Baale Jaha. "Perhaps . . . we should not—"

"No!" Ashâke wiped angrily at her tears. "No. I want to know. If the orisha are . . ." She took a deep breath. "I want to know. *Please.*"

A moment passed in which the griots exchanged meaningful looks, then—

"Very well," said Jaha. "We will Sing you a Song. We will Sing of the Fall of the Orisha."

A change came upon the air. Ashâke could not tell where the instruments came from, but the griots were suddenly bearing koras and shakers, gongs and flutes and cowhide drums. They rose slowly to their feet and arranged themselves in a circle around her. Then Djola stepped into the circle, a massive batá drum hanging around his neck. He struck it once and a boom cracked the night, like a clap of thunder. He let the sound peter out before striking the drum again, and again, and again, coaxing a hypnotic, throbbing rhythm: DUM-dum-dum. DUM-dum-dum.

The koras came alive, strings shaking out warm chords; the flutes joined, their sombre melodies weaving through the chords, and the griots lifted their voices as one, blending in sweet, sweet harmony until there was an aural backdrop for the Master Griot to Sing.

Jaha stepped into the circle, spread his ample arms wide, and bellowed to the heavens:

"In the land above the sky
Lived the Lord of all beings;
Olodumare, Father of orisha and men.

For ages man lived, oblivious to the existence of the orisha,
Stumbling through life like children in a swamp.
Olodumare sought to reveal astral mysteries to men
So He called forth the orisha from the corners of the world
And bade them build a bridge;
A tower, a gateway to link the realms of man and orisha."

The world fell away. The griots, the trees, the fire. Everything dissolved in a swirl of colours, as though reality were merely a painter's impression on a clay tablet, washed away by water. Ashâke was all alone in a dark, formless space. Still she heard their voices, heard the music, heard the Master Griot's sonorous chant. Then the world burst into colour before her, and she found herself before a tall, tapering structure. Ashâke knew it on sight, from depictions in the temple: the Tower of the Orisha, connecting Aye to Orun.

"The orisha worked together and built the Tower:
Ogun, orisha of metal, provided the tools for construction;
Shango, orisha of fire and thunder and lightning,
Shattered the Mountains of Abeokuta with lightning
The rocks of which were used to build the Tower;
Yemoja, mother of the seas and rain

Held off rainfall while it was built.
Several seasons passed, and when Oganju, the orisha of completion
Set the final stone in place, there was rejoicing and merriment
In all the land."

The music took on a lively tempo as the scene dissolved into another. Ashâke made out several shapes caught in the throes of revelry: countless people, dancing at the foot of the Tower. Among them stood towering figures, effusing a powerful aura: orisha.

"The Tower was completed; now there could be direct
Communication between man and orisha as Olodumare
Had always wanted.
Every season before the rains, the Afin and his griots and select citizens
Of the kingdom could ascend through the Tower to Orun itself
To partake in a Conclave of orisha and men.
The orisha taught man the secrets of divination,
How to divine the message of the orisha through the arbitrary placement
Of cowrie shells across divination boards.
They taught men the invocations, the two hundred and fifty-six odu ifa,

Gifting man with the knowledge to successfully
navigate the world.
These men became priests of Ifa."

Ashâke glimpsed several men and women garbed in white priestly raiment, hunched over divination boards, casting cowries. But for the striking, imposing figures of the orisha hovering above them, it could have been the temple. *Her* temple, where she had tried tirelessly to get the orisha to speak to her. For a moment she imagined herself one of the priests, bursting with joy as the orisha taught her the language of divination. Oh, how she would have cherished their instruction, basked in their attention.

The scene changed, and the music took on an urgent, dramatic tone.

"The Fall of the Orisha came in the nineteenth season
Of Alafin Tade the Third.
The Afin, with his griots, the High Priest, and select
citizens
Ascended the Tower to Orun.
Little did they know that among their numbers was
a sect.
A secret cult with a dark motive. A cult whose name
would ring forever
On the lips of posterity:
Godkillers."

Ashâke shuddered. That word. It defied everything she knew. She could hardly fathom how mere men could possess the power to kill orisha.

Around her arose spectres of men, hooded man-shaped shadows, and she knew them for what they were. God-killers. Faceless, unknowable, bane of the orisha.

"The Conclave opened with a feast as was custom.
There was merriment. There was music. There was laughter.
Olodumare sat in his throne at the head of the table, surrounded by the orisha,
And his mortal children, and thought to himself that he had done well.
As the feast drew to an end, a man arose and called loudly across the hall:
'Olodumare, baba mi, permission to approach your throne. I have a gift for you!'
The Supreme Father, terribly pleased, waved him over."

A man rose from the table and strode slowly towards the throne. His dark ebon skin seemed almost radiant, as though he were himself an orisha. A terrible scar raked his face, claiming his left eye. His golden hair grew into seven thick locs, which spilled over his shoulders.

His intent was written all over him, in the twist of his

lips and the set of his chin. How could the orisha have missed it? How could Olodumare himself have missed it?

The voice of the Master Griot boomed through the walls:

"The man went on one knee before Olodumare who said,
'Tell me, son, what is your name?'
'I am Bahl'ul. But my followers call me Teacher.'
Olodumare, amused, said, 'And what have you for me, Teacher?'
At this point, the man looked Olodumare in the eye and hissed: 'Death.'
In one swift, fluid movement, Bahl'ul rose to his feet, and produced a terrible black
Scimitar from the fold of his robes. Olodumare's eyes widened and he reached for His scepter.
Too late: Bahl'ul ran the Supreme Father through with his blade and Olodumare fell
Back on his throne, wheezing, gawking in disbelief at the aberration in his breast, at
The jagged lines of bright light rapidly spreading over his arms, his face . . .
Olodumare exploded. Dead."

It took Ashâke a moment to realise that the howl of anguish belonged to her. The Creator was dead, had been dead many seasons, but her pain was true. Tears poured down her cheeks, as the godkiller turned to regard the stunned faces of orisha and men alike.

"Other figures rose from among the seated:
Figures dressed in red, the followers of Bahl'ul,
wielding terrible blades of destruction.
They laid waste to the inebriated orisha.
Pandemonium reigned."

The screams. Stars above, the screams. They rang with terror, betrayal, pain. And Ashâke felt every one of them, every single roiling emotion.

"The orisha fled, or tried to flee, but they were no
match for the followers of the Teacher.
Their senses were dulled by an excess of wine and
sweet food.
All but Shango.
The lord of fire and thunder and lightning arose with
great fury
And visited the vengeance of the orisha upon them.
Lightning rocked Orun as he swung his double-
headed axe in blind rage, felling his foes.
And innocents in the process.
The Afin fell, as did griots and priests.
So great was Shango's rage that he very nearly
destroyed the world.
But Orun was not enough to contain his fury, and

the Seat of the Orisha went up in flames, even as the Tower shattered, and Shango, lord of thunder and fire and lightning, was consumed by his own fury."

Shango's terrible form blossomed before Ashâke, his eyes burning coals as he tore through Orun, sweeping with his great axe, belching fire like an enraged kulukaya, sending bolts of red lightning at friend and foe alike.

Shango stood alone among a heap of dead bodies, many of whom were his siblings. His shoulders heaved as he stared at what had become of them. His eyes roved over Ashâke, and though he was not really here, though he was not really looking at her, she shrank back from the weight of that terrible regard. He raised his axe far above his head and *screamed*: fire sprang from his mouth, red and yellow and orange, even as Orun exploded in a brilliant spray of colours.

The scene changed, showing the Tower, dark and formidable, rising up into the sky, into Orun. For a moment it stood as it had for thousands of seasons. Then, several bolts of red lightning fractured the heavens. They lit the night sky, terrible in their beauty, illuminating far longer than any lightning should. A bolt forked through the Tower. The top half shifted, teetered on its edge, then with a great groan, shattered.

A great earthquake rocked the continent. Trees were torn up by their roots. Deep cracks forked through the earth, widening into rifts and gullies and deep, deep channels. The sea rushed into the channels, widening them, pushing apart the chunks of land that would become the Ten Kingdoms. Cities fell into the sea, settlements and villages gobbled whole by the hungry waters. Children screamed for their mothers, and wives shrieked for their husbands, who called for their own mothers. All of them, man and woman and child, screamed for the orisha to save them.

But the orisha were dead and could not save them.

Ashâke hugged her knees to her chest as she stared into the fire, tears streaming down her face. The orisha had opened Orun to man, and what did he do? Kill them. But why? What motivated Bahl'ul and his followers? What power did they possess that granted them the ability to kill orisha?

Godkillers, the Master Griot had called them. Ashâke shuddered.

She did not notice when the griots stopped singing, when they retired to their tents. She could not tell who, but someone had wrapped her in a blanket, and she pulled it tighter about herself as she watched the fire burn down to glowing coals, watched the embers turn to white ash.

Sometime in the long night Mama Agba approached and fed more wood into the fire. Then she sat next to her.

"I realise this must be difficult for you," she said. "To have your faith so very terribly shaken."

Ashâke snorted, wiped the snot from her nose. "It isn't shaken. It is lost. Everything I thought I knew . . . why would they *do* it? Why would the priests pretend that the orisha still live? How does that *help* anyone?"

"We all cope in different ways," she said. "In my time I have come across many priests. But it takes a special kind of delusion to ignore that which is so clearly before you."

Or a special kind of dedication to a lie.

"That's why they keep us hidden away as youths, so we don't learn the truth. Until we are conditioned so well that we can go into the world, hear about the Fall and not waver in our faith."

"You are free now. Free to see the world for yourself and make of it what you will." Mama Agba sighed. "The Fall of the Orisha happened four hundred seasons ago, and the aftermath was terrible. The world devolved into chaos. The established order of things suddenly and without warning ceased to exist. We became children without parents. Half the world destroyed, the continent split into several islands. Worse was the frightful notion that our orisha were fallible, that among us were people capable *and* willing to kill them."

The image of Bahl'ul bloomed in Ashâke's mind, as he stabbed Olodumare. She shuddered. "Who are they, these people? How are they so . . . powerful?"

Mama Agba looked suddenly older in the firelight. "Many have asked that question. No one knows."

They sat there in silence, staring out at the mist-cloaked

river and the boats. Someone coughed in their sleep. Okoye, the night's watchman, slinked out of the forest, silent as a panther. He nodded at Mama Agba, who greeted him.

"Gaza's boat has been repaired," said the woman to Ashâke. "We sail for Inysha on the morrow. Try to get some rest."

With that the matriarch stood, leaving Ashâke to her thoughts.

EIGHT

At the hour of the jackal, Ashâke finally stumbled from her perch by the fire and made her way towards her tent.

Someone was lying face down in the dirt.

Her heart froze even as her mind went blank. They lay some distance from the camp, where the bank gave way to thick forest. Ashâke's first thought was that someone had woken up for a midnight piss and had collapsed in a drunken stupor. But then she saw the spear, lying two strides from his outstretched hand, she saw the white bracelet that marked him as a watchman, saw the long, curved scar on his arm.

"Djola!" she cried, rushing towards him. *"Djola!"*

His head flopped uselessly in her arms, and she patted him over, searching for a wound, a swell, anything to suggest that he had taken a blow to the head. But she found nothing. He seemed to have simply collapsed. She put her hand beneath his nose and gave a shudder of relief when she felt his warm breath. He was alive.

Something moved in the corner of her eye, and Ashâke found herself diving for the spear, leaping into a crouch as a figure stepped from the shadows.

They wore a kaftan of midnight blue, inlaid with sacred

shells, a white horsetail whisk hanging from their sash, their face hidden behind a bronze mask Ashâke would recognise anywhere.

"High Priestess," she breathed.

It was hard to break with seasons of conditioning. Even though her mind screamed at her to run, Ashâke found herself bowing in reverence, touching forehead to mud.

"Rise, child."

Ashâke rose to her feet and faced the High Priestess.

Iyalawo looked down at Djola's unconscious form. "The ashe is strong in him, as it is in all griots. I cloaked myself and though he could not see me, he still sensed my presence. So I put him to sleep. I put all the watchmen to sleep." She turned back to Ashâke. "I've come to take you back to where you belong."

Once upon a time, those words, coming from the High Priestess herself, would have sent Ashâke into unimaginable fits of rapture. Once, she would have screamed and danced and laughed at the very idea that she belonged, that she was needed. Now she knew the truth, and it felt like she was being offered an empty coconut.

"No."

Iyalawo cocked her head, her mask as expressionless as ever, as intimidating as ever. "No?"

Ashâke swallowed. "No. I won't go back to a life of ridicule and empty yearning and *lies*! Not now that I know that the orisha are dead!"

Silence. It hung heavy over the clearing, wound tight around Ashâke's throat.

"When did you learn of this?" asked Iyalawo.

"So it's true, then. You've been lying to us—"

"When?"

"An hour, two hours ago," said Ashâke. "What does it matter?"

"Oh, you fool child." The High Priestess offered her hand. "We must leave at once."

"Did you not hear me? I said I'm not—"

"You think you know it all, but you don't. You really don't. We must go. Now."

"No! I won't—"

"Come."

The word came at her from all sides, rang loud in her ears, as though the wind had carried the voices of a rabble chanting that one word. A command. Ashâke felt it take possession of her body, set her feet into motion.

"What are you doing?" cried Ashâke as her feet carried her over Djola and towards the High Priestess. "Let me go! Let me—Help! DJOLA! WAKE UP! MAMA AGBA! *HELP!*"

"Silence."

Ashâke's mouth moved but no sound issued forth. The High Priestess had stolen her voice, rendering her a prisoner in her own body, unable to scream, unable to struggle. A sheep following her master. Ashâke had never hated anyone as much as she did as she cantered after Iyalawo, away from the griots and deeper into the forest.

Iyalawo unhooked the horsetail whisk from her sash and flicked it. It burst into flames, and she held it aloft like a torch. Ashâke gazed in wonder as it burned but was not consumed by the fire. Such open displays of magic were rare.

Deeper into the forest they went, past bamboo groves and a stinking swamp, until finally they came before a cave. This was evidently not the temple. Why were they here? The High Priestess stood staring at the dark space that was the entrance. Ashâke frowned at her in question, but Iyalawo ignored her as her legs carried her into the cave.

Inside, darkness. And a biting chill. Ashâke stood there wondering how large the cave was, contemplating all the numerous ways she could die. She could not help but think that Iyalawo had brought her here to die. She could starve to death, trapped in her own skin, unable to scream for help. How long would it take for her body to be found, if ever it was found? Perhaps many seasons later some hunter seeking shelter would come upon it, and make weapons from her bones.

Iyalawo entered the cave. She walked about, flaming whisk aloft, casting into light the pocked walls and vine-covered roof and a huge gnarled root that tore through the west wall. It seemed she was searching for something, for she passed her hands over the walls, muttering under her breath. Satisfied, she tied a dried vine to the handle of her whisk so that it dangled from the roof, illuminating the cave. Then she turned her attention on Ashâke.

"We can speak here," she said.

Ashâke felt whatever power the High Priestess used to bind her vanish as she regained control of her body. Her first thought was to bolt. But by accident or design the High Priestess was blocking her only path to exit. Not to mention that with one word she could easily lock Ashâke's limbs again, rendering her a prisoner in her own body once more, and who knew if she would be released this time? The woman clearly wanted to speak, so speak they would. Ashâke took a deep breath.

"Why are we here?" she asked. "I thought you were taking me to the temple."

"We cannot return just yet," said Iyalawo. "You have lost your faith."

"Faith? You mean I'm no longer one of your many sheep, gobbling down your lies. What are you going to do to me?" Ashâke inched backwards. "I know the truth so you're going to kill me, is that it?"

"You do not know the truth. You know at best a half-truth."

"I know the orisha are dead."

"True, the Fall of the Orisha happened. True, many orisha perished on that day." Iyalawo paused. "But not all of them."

Ashâke squinted in suspicion. "What do you mean, not all of them? The griots—"

"Do not know everything."

"And you do?"

"Yes. Yes, I do."

"I don't believe you."

The High Priestess sighed, her shoulders sagging. Ashâke had never seen her look quite so . . . diminished. "No," she said quietly. "I suppose you don't." And then she reached behind her head, working her hands at something. It took Ashâke a moment to realise what she was doing, but by then it was too late; the High Priestess had unfastened the clasps that held up her mask, peeling it away to reveal her face.

Ashâke looked away.

"Look at me," said Iyalawo. Ashâke stared at the floor, heat crawling up her neck. She felt like she had stumbled upon the woman's nakedness. As far as Ashâke knew, no one had looked upon the face of the High Priestess in a long time, and she couldn't fathom why she was now revealing her face. "Child. Look at me."

Reluctantly, Ashâke looked, gasping at the sight before her.

Iyalawo's face was burnt. Half the High Priestess's face and the parts of her neck Ashâke could see were mottled, as though eaten by flames. Her left ear was so shrivelled it looked like a wilted cauliflower. But perhaps what was most shocking was that she did not look much older than

Ashâke. Perhaps by three or four seasons. She could be her older sister.

"The Flame of Shango is all-consuming," said Iyalawo, rolling up her sleeves to show arms just as burnt, just as mottled. "The orisha could barely put me back together."

"The Flame of Shango." Ashâke frowned. "I don't understand . . . why would Shango attack you?"

"His attack wasn't directed at me; I was merely unfortunate enough to be in his vicinity."

That sounded like Shango. Hadn't she just seen in Song and Memory the result of his rage? Hadn't she watched, horrified, as he belched fire at friend and foe—?

"Wait a moment." Ashâke took in Iyalawo's mottled skin, her singed scalp, and her mouth went dry. "You were there . . ." she breathed. "You—you *saw* the Fall!"

"I did."

"But . . . but that was four hundred *seasons* ago! How is that even . . . ?"

"The orisha had a vested interest in my survival . . . because I possessed something of great value, something that they desperately needed."

"What?" Ashâke whispered. "What did the orisha need from you?"

Iyalawo gave a sad smile. She began to pace, slowly, her kaftan rustling over the cave floor. "You know of how Bahl'ul and his followers attacked the orisha and how Shango visited his vengeance on them. What you don't know is that some orisha escaped. Fled to Aye. But this world is not for orisha . . . especially with Olodumare dead and the"—she bit off the word—"*godkillers* at large. The essence of the Supreme Father was shattered into fragments, with Bahl'ul's followers claiming parts for themselves, granting them incomprehensible power. The orisha could not survive on Aye, not in their diminished form. They could not battle their enemy, so they made one last, desperate effort to save themselves. They made a Guardian."

"A Guardian?" asked Ashâke.

"In truth, an idan."

Ashâke frowned. "A clay life-form, like I tried to make?"

"An idan can be many things," said Iyalawo. "It is we mortals who in crafting an idan make use of the tools at hand. We use clay, the raw substance from which Obatala formed us. To house their divine spirit, the orisha chose a thing of bone and flesh and blood, given life by their actions."

"A person?"

"Yes," continued Iyalawo. "But the enemy is crafty. With the location of the orisha and their idan hidden away, the killers turned to another mode of warfare: a war of belief. The orisha can only truly exist if they burn bright in the minds of their followers. And so for many, many seasons the priests of Ifa have waged a war of belief against Bahl'ul and his followers, who have insinuated themselves into every level of society, spreading the lie that the orisha are dead." She sighed. "It is a war we are struggling to win. If enough people believe that the orisha are dead, then they will truly die. The orisha hang on to life through our unwavering belief in them—the few of us who believe, anyway."

"You say the . . . godkillers have insinuated themselves into every level of society. Could they . . ." She feared to ask the question, was not even certain she wanted the answer, but Iyalawo caught her meaning.

"They could be anyone. And that is what makes them dangerous. The followers have mastered the art of disguise. You can never know if your neighbour is one of them. Their ears are everywhere, their eyes are everywhere, searching for the Guardian. But this . . . what I have told you, is the secret I reveal to acolytes upon accession into priesthood, so that they can go out in the world, armed with the knowledge of the truth and battle every lie whispered by the followers of Bahl'ul."

How convenient that Iyalawo revealed this knowledge only to newly acceded priests. How could Ashâke, who had never acceded, confirm its veracity? How could the other acolytes? No. She would not be so easily fooled. This woman had lied to her all her life. She could be lying right now. "If the orisha are not dead, why can't I hear them?"

Iyalawo had a strange look in her eyes. "Ashâke," she said softly. "Do you know why acolytes are forbidden from leaving the temple without senior priests?"

"To keep us from learning the truth."

"To prevent contact with a disbelieving outsider. An ancient magic shields the temple, protects it from the godkillers. And that magic is held up by our collective belief in the orisha."

"That does not answer my question. Why can't *I* hear the orisha? And why do you need to shield the temple?"

"Because, Ashâke, the Guardian dwells within the walls of the temple. And should the followers ever learn of its location, then they will come, in their hundreds, in their thousands, to finish what they started."

Ashâke frowned. "The Guardian . . . dwells within the temple?" She looked up at Iyalawo, into those old, knowing eyes, into that burned face pieced back together by the orisha, and staggered backwards with the weight of realisation. "It's you," she breathed.

It made all the sense in the world. Why else would the orisha piece her back? How else had she lived so long?

Iyalawo shook her head. "No, child." She stepped closer, until Ashâke could feel the heat rising off her skin. "An acolyte held back while her peers acceded," she whispered. "An acolyte frustrated because she thinks she is unable to hear the orisha and feels abandoned by them. An acolyte safer behind the magic of the temple than out in the world where followers of Bahl'ul loom at large."

Ashâke heard the words, understood their implication, yet could not quite bring herself to acknowledge them.

"You cannot truly be deaf to the orisha," whispered Iyalawo, "for you *are* the orisha."

"No," croaked Ashâke, finding her voice at last. "You're wrong. It is impossible. I can't even—"

Iyalawo seized her by the shoulders and blew *hard* into her face. Ashâke's head snapped backwards as air rushed in through her nostrils. Heat flared through her body, and a high keening sound filled her ears.

She staggered backwards, grasping wildly as the cave spun. Iyalawo's voice came as if from the bottom of a well, distant and hollow:

". . . I made a grave mistake . . . you were just a child, I couldn't bring myself to let you go."

Ashâke dropped to her knees, gasping. Intricate symbols appeared on her skin, etchings of ancient glyphs carved into every inch of flesh.

It was the language of Orun, the language of binding, and strangely, strangely, she knew it.

Ashâke's mind exploded with images.

She saw it all.

INTERLUDE III

FOUR HUNDRED SEASONS AGO

Pain. Rombi was aware of a terrible blooming pain as she came to. She moaned. Her tongue was on fire, her mouth parched. She cracked open her eyes, trying to remember where she was, how she'd come to be here. There had been . . . a feast, yes, with the orisha and—

The killers!

She sat up, howled as the sudden movement sent waves of pain crashing over her.

"Don't move so suddenly," said a voice. A woman. Through the haze of pain Rombi saw the figure leaning over her, pressing her to the bed. She had a full head of white hair that shaped her brown face like a halo, and her eyes . . . her eyes were the shifting hues of the seas, of a sky pregnant with rainfall.

"Yemoja," she gasped.

"Very good, daughter," said the orisha of seas and fertility. "Very good."

"Am I dead?"

"Not anymore."

Not any . . . ? Rombi twisted on the bed. Her skin was sticky with sweat. She was in a vast hall with massive, sweeping arches and alabaster white columns. Sunlight fell in huge shafts through rectangular slits in the walls and ceiling, illuminating the floor. This was not Orun. Orun was in ruins, ablaze, piled high with the bodies of dead orisha. She had seen them all fall. How was Yemoja alive? How was *she* alive?

She remembered the madness in Shango's eyes, a terrifying thing, because without his wife, without his voice of reason, there had been no one to temper his rage. She remembered his flames licking her, she remembered the way her skin had bubbled, sloughing off her bones while she screamed, begging for her—

"My baby!" she cried, feeling for the swell of her belly. "My *baby*."

"Easy, child," said Yemoja. "She's coming. You must push. Do you hear me? Push."

Rombi pushed, a terrible wail tearing out her throat. She pushed, howling as pain spasmed through her back and sex. Stars above, it hurt. It hurt so much. Her hand found the orisha's and she gripped it hard, wanting to pass over the hurt, willing her to take away the pain.

Yemoja was smiling down at her, aglow, and though her lips did not move, Rombi heard her voice, her song, loud in her head . . .

She was a little girl again, sprinting in the rain, running away from home and her baba's wicked new wife. It was so dark, so hard to make out anything, so she didn't see that she was racing towards a cliff, didn't realise until it was too late, and the ground vanished beneath her feet.

The wind ate her voice as she tumbled through the air. Then—cold. A biting, shocking cold as she splashed into the water, sucked under by the turbulent currents. Her head broke the surface, once, twice, but the water had a mind of its own, and soon she was drowning, unable to tell up from down, the cold black water flooding her lungs.

I don't want to die, *she thought.* Please, I don't want to die.

And then she heard the song. A calming melody in her head that soothed her thrashing. She saw the orisha, a beacon in the dark waters as she swam towards her, plucking her from the river's turbulent grip and bearing her to shore.

Rombi lay on the muddy bank, gaping in awe at the orisha, delirious, grateful. "Thank you, mother of the seas," she said. "My heart is yours. My life is yours. Now and forever."

Rombi shuddered as she was pulled back to the present. Yemoja knelt between her legs, cradling a bloody bundle in her arms. A strangled cry escaped her lips, one of pain, of relief, of exhaustion. The orisha had seen her through the pain of childbirth. Rombi looked from the child—her child—to the orisha.

"Why isn't . . . why isn't she crying?" she said, her voice catching with panic. "Why isn't she moving?"

"Shhh." Yemoja pressed a hand to her forehead. "Sleep. Sleep . . ."

Rombi slept.

It was dark when she came to a second time. The shafts of light coming through the slits were now silver moonlight, playing across the patterned floor. In the very centre of the hall, fire burned in a crucible. Rombi's heart raced at the sight of those tall flames.

She sat up. She had been cleaned, and dressed in a loose floral gown. Her arms were bare so that her mottled skin was exposed. She passed her hands over it, feeling the unevenness of it. No one should survive such a thing. But then she hadn't. She had died . . . and so had her child.

Her *child*.

Rombi flew out of the bed, casting around the hall. "Hello?" she called. "Orisha iya mi?"

Her voice washed out across the hall. Where was she? And where was Yemoja? Had she hallucinated her childbirth? No. The hall was the same, and she knew she had been pregnant.

She started across the hall.

There were several doors, each one of them closed, some without even a handle. And just when she was starting to despair, she heard the cry of a babe, and she hurried out of the chamber and into the courtyard beyond.

Yemoja sat in a swing, cradling a bundle, her white hair

billowing about her. The swing hung from the limb of a massive white baobab, which leaned out to the world below.

Rombi let out a strangled cry at the sight of her baby, at the sight of those searching eyes. She was alive. Her child was alive.

Yemoja smiled up at her. "Come. Sit. And meet your child."

Rombi sank onto the swing next to Yemoja and the orisha placed the babe carefully in her arms. Rombi thought her heart would burst with joy.

"Thank you," she whispered, tears leaking down her cheeks. "Thank you."

She was so warm, so small, so . . . in need of protection. The babe stared at her with huge brown eyes, and satisfied with what she saw, reached out a chubby hand to pat Rombi's cheek, cooing softly. Rombi laughed. There was nothing she wouldn't do to protect this child. She would without a moment's hesitation trade her own happiness if that would keep her daughter safe.

"Such a precious little thing, isn't she?" said Yemoja. "Children. They are so innocent, so helpless. It is when they grow that you must watch them, before they think to reach beyond their station, and become a thorn in your side, before they forget those who gave them life."

She said it calmly enough, pleasantly enough, but Rombi felt the change in the air. The wind grew chillier, and a crushing weight came upon her. It felt as though she were being trampled by a dozen enraged elephants. She could hardly draw breath, and even her daughter started to fuss, wheezing. When Rombi looked at Yemoja, the orisha's eyes had turned to glowing chips of ice, whatever warmth lay there evaporated. Her white hair came alive, ballooning out, the strands writhing like a thousand tiny worms. Rombi realised with horror that she was shedding her mortal form. There was a reason why the orisha never showed their true essence to mortals; to behold their true form was to be unmade, the very threads of your mind unraveled. Rombi opened her mouth, even though that was a struggle, even though it felt as though she were being crushed beneath the weight of a mountain, and gasped "Mother—"

Yemoja closed her eyes and sighed, and the pressure was gone, the biting cold vanished, and she was her usual pleasant self.

"Forgive me," said the orisha. "I am wrathful . . . I am tired."

"You speak of . . . the killers?" Rombi licked her lips, holding her baby tighter. "The other orisha. Are they . . ."

"The orisha are asleep," said Yemoja. "Those not dead at least. They cannot manifest for long. The enemies dealt a terrible blow. Olodumare is dead, and without him we can't . . . they *stole* his essence, divvied it amongst themselves like pieces of game. They made a mockery of us . . ."

A fine crack ran through her cheek, as though she were a piece of sculpture succumbing to the elements.

"Your . . . your face," said Rombi.

Yemoja's face began to flake, tiny brown pieces crumbling off. She caught some in her palm and stared as they dissolved into glowing dust and then into nothing. "I, too, must slumber. I have . . . spent myself too much, but I fear even that is not enough. The veil I've erected around this temple shields us from their eyes, but I cannot hold it for long. The killers will not stop until every orisha is dead."

"Why?"

"I, too, would like to know that. I would like to know that very much."

Yemoja looked down at the clouds, and the vast darkness of the firmament. "Down there word is spreading of what happened and our followers and ardents are beginning to lose faith. What use is an orisha without the prayers of their acolytes? What use is an orisha who is forgotten?"

They died. That was the first thing they were taught as acolytes. The orisha thrived on prayers and devotion, rewarding their most ardent devotees. Rombi shuddered. She could not fathom that the Supreme Father was dead. She could not imagine what kind of power the killers possessed that they could so easily fell even one of the orisha.

"What will you do?"

"Hunt them. These thieves, these usurpers, these *killers*. We must know how they came about their powers. We must know why they are determined to finish us off."

"But how? You say you need to slumber. You cannot face . . . these killers yet."

Yemoja gave her a meaningful smile. "Not like this, we can't."

Rombi understood now, why she had been saved, why she had been brought here.

"Take me," she said. "Use me as your vessel. Your idan."

"All of us in you, you couldn't handle it. For this to work, we will need a vessel filled with pure ashe. A mind yet unformed, and pliant to our needs . . ." Her eyes went down to the baby.

Rombi gripped her child as terror racked her body. "No," she said, then remembered who she was talking to. "I mean . . . please . . . is this why you brought me here? You rescued me because you knew—you knew it would come to this."

The orisha's gaze was intense, unflinching. "Many seasons ago, you pledged your life to me, 'now and forever,' do you remember?"

Of course, she remembered. How could she forget? Hadn't she dedicated her entire life to service?

"Yes, but not the life—not the life of my daughter."

"All life belongs to me." Yemoja put a hand on the baby's head, smoothing her curls. "This miracle is my doing."

"She'll be hunted. The killers, they won't stop—*please* . . ."

"She will survive because I am with her, we will all be with her."

Rombi held her child close. She had fallen asleep now,

her tiny chest rising and falling as she breathed. What kind of a life would she have, forever fleeing killers, seeking answers? There was no guarantee she wouldn't be killed. These were the same nameless, faceless people who had murdered the Supreme Father as though he were nothing. Rombi thought of running off the cliff, plunging to her death with her child. But Yemoja wouldn't let them go so easily. She had no choice in the matter. What the orisha demanded you gave without question.

Weeping, she handed over the child.

Yemoja cradled the babe in the crook of one arm, making soothing sounds as she adjusted her wrappings with the other. She touched a finger to the child's forehead and the etchings appeared, spreading from that one spot to cover every inch of her skin: intricate whorls and glyphs, the language of binding. They began to glow a faint blue as though within her was contained a bright light.

"You have not named her," said the orisha. "What would you like to call her?"

"Ashâke."

The goddess smiled. "A fitting name. 'Chosen of the orisha. Guardian of the gods.'"

"And you." She wiped at Rombi's tears, then touched a thumb to her forehead. "For your sacrifice, for your devotion, I name you Iyalawo: High Priestess of the Orisha, Mother of Mysteries."

With that she stood and glided towards the hall, singing a lullaby to the sleeping child.

NINE

Ashâke gaped at Iyalawo, speechless. The High Priestess knelt before her, lips trembling, tears leaking down her ruined face.

"I'm sorry," Iyalawo sobbed. "I'm so, so sorry. For all you've had to go through, all you've had to suffer, thinking that you were not loved, that you were not wanted. When in truth . . ." She took a deep, shuddering breath. "I wanted you too much to let go. I was . . . selfish. I wanted you with me. So once the ritual was complete and their essence had been transferred to you, I subdued them, and made you forget. I thought if we could get enough people to believe then the orisha wouldn't need you, then they would leave you to me. I thought . . ." She broke into fresh tears.

All this while her mother had been within arm's reach, and she'd been none the wiser. But hadn't she felt, over the seasons, that she was being watched? How often while praying or doing some task had she felt eyes on her, only to look up and find no one? But she had never been alone. Iyalawo had always been there, in the shadows, watching over her.

"You . . . are my mother . . ." The words were odd to hear, stranger even in her mouth. But it was true.

"I didn't wear a mask to hide my scars," said Iyalawo.

"I wore a mask to hide our similarities. Any fool could have looked at you, and looked at me, and guessed what we were."

Mother and daughter.

Ashâke threw herself at Iyalawo and crushed her in a hug, holding her so tightly, so hard her ribs hurt. But she never let go. And when she felt Iyalawo's arms encircle her, holding her just as tightly, it was all she could do not to weep.

For so long she had felt utterly alone. For so long she had remained friendless, aching to hear the orisha, yearning to become a priest. But she hadn't come to the temple to become a priest. She was the Guardian. The orisha dwelt within her. Even now she felt them, felt them in her mind in a way she hadn't before. It was as though she shared her mind with several others. And she did. Truly, she did.

"I felt them," she said. "That night when I tried to summon Eshu. I heard their voices, I felt them in my mind."

Iyalawo nodded. "You almost set them loose. There is a lot I have to tell you, a lot I must teach you—"

"Wait a moment," said Ashâke, frowning. "If the Fall was four hundred seasons ago, that means . . ." She searched Iyalawo's eyes. "That means *I* am four hundred seasons old! *How?* I only have memories of these past two and twenty seasons."

"I put you into deep slumber—although we cannot exactly call it slumber. It was more a state of arrested animation. I needed time to work out how to subdue the orisha." She cupped Ashâke's face. "It is no easy thing to trap one orisha, let alone several. But they were vulnerable, greatly weakened, and they had surrendered themselves to you." She shrugged, her shoulders shifting beneath her thin kaftan. "So I did what I had to do to keep you safe, to keep you with me."

Ashâke cupped Iyalawo's face, and leaned in close, so that they were touching foreheads. "You did what any mother would do," she whispered.

Iyalawo gave her a watery smile. "But now they must be awakened. And Yemoja will not forgive my meddling . . ." She trailed off.

"What?" asked Ashâke. "What's wrong? I will intercede on your behalf if that's what—"

Iyalawo rose abruptly to her feet. "We are not alone." She untied her flaming horsetail whisk from where it hung. "Wait here." And she turned and swept for the cave mouth. Ashâke scrambled to her feet after her.

Dawn was fast approaching, and there was just enough twilight filtering through the trees to illuminate the boy standing in front of the cave, arms clasped behind his back as he waited patiently.

"I told you to stay back!" Iyalawo hissed as Ashâke came to her side.

"It's fine!" said Ashâke. "He's one of the griots." She cast around to see if there were any more of them. "They're probably searching for me."

"That," said Iyalawo, biting off each word, "is not a griot. He is a *godkiller.*"

A cold current travelled down Ashâke's spine. "Are you . . . are you sure?" But she saw it in his eyes, in the set of his shoulders.

They insinuate themselves into every level of society. Weren't the griots, who took in folk without question or judgment, who travelled far and wide across the Ten Kingdoms, perfectly suited to do this? Ashâke recalled with growing terror how the boy had ambushed her, demanding to know the whereabouts of the temple. He had been searching for her, even though she hadn't known it, even though *he* hadn't known it. And now he'd found her. "Stars above," she said weakly.

"Godkiller." The boy's mouth twisted in distaste. "How I abhor that shallow label. We are much, much more. I am Yaruddin, servant of the Great Teacher Bahl'ul."

"Leave, godkiller." Iyalawo's lips pulled back in a sneer. "Your kind are not welcome here."

Yaruddin took a step forward, only to come up against an invisible barrier. Frowning, he put a hand into the air, testing the barrier, and an iridescent bubble shimmered into view. It enveloped the entire cave.

His hand burst into flames.

Yaruddin pulled it back, frowned down at it, as though it were not ablaze, as though it were a mere annoyance, then quietly smothered the flames with his other hand.

"A warding," he said. "How . . . quaint. Surely you must know you cannot stop me. Nor can you defeat me." His empty eyes slid to Ashâke and back to Iyalawo. "Hand over the Guardian and you need not die."

"Leave this place at once and *you* need not die," Iyalawo returned.

Ashâke wiped her clammy hands on her clothes, breathing hard and fast. She wanted to run. She wanted to run as far away from here as possible. But they were trapped, and there was nowhere to go. Visions of the Fall burned bright in her mind, visions of Bahl'ul's followers laying waste to the orisha, the shock on Olodumare's face as he died. They were no match for these people. How could Iyalawo stand brave before such a one?

Yaruddin stretched a hand to his side and a cloud of purple-black mist swirled about it, slowly condensing into a black scimitar, the very kind that had obliterated the Supreme Father. Ashâke felt her knees grow weak with fresh terror.

He raised it up and sliced the air. There came a high-pitched clang as it struck the warding, sparks flying off at the point of impact. The shield shimmered as cracks spidered through it. Several birds took flight, their dark shapes fluttering over the trees into the lightening morning. Yaruddin struck again and again and again.

With each blow the cave shuddered, clumps of putrid earth breaking off the roof to collapse in a pall of dust on the floor. Ashâke looked in alarm to see cracks appear in the roof and walls. The cave was dangerously close to falling in.

"Guardian!" called the godkiller. "There is nowhere for you to go! There is no place where you might hide where we won't find you!"

Iyalawo turned to Ashâke. "Listen to me. This warding will not hold. Once it breaks, I want you to race for the temple—"

"What?"

"I will keep him occupied. Bahl'ul's followers are unable to enter the temple, and it will remain that way as long as your belief is strong and you continue to believe."

"No!" Ashâke gripped her hands. "You cannot face him. He'll kill you!"

Iyalawo smiled. "They took the orisha unawares; I have had four hundred seasons to prepare for this moment."

The warding winked once, twice, then vanished. Gone.

Iyalawo raised her whisk. "You will not take the orisha," she boomed. "And you will not take my child."

A spear came whistling out of the trees. It sailed fast through the air and took Yaruddin square in the back. He flew forwards, buoyed by the spear's momentum, arms splayed as if to hug the air. He landed on his knees, propped up by the bloody spearhead jutting out of his chest, black blood soaking his clothes. The scimitar vanished from his hand, dissolving in a swirl of black mist.

Someone came tearing out of the trees.

"Djola!" called Ashâke.

"It's alright!" he yelled. "The others . . ."

A cloud of mist seeped out of the body. Ashâke thought at first it was the scimitar, but it did not condense into a solid shape. It remained instead a swirling, amorphous substance hovering above Yaruddin's lifeless body.

Ashâke felt a tugging in the pit of her belly, as though a lasso had been thrown around her midriff, yanking at her. She started forwards.

She felt Iyalawo's hand clamp around her shoulder and the woman's hot breath in her ear. *"Run!"*

But she could not run. She felt herself drawn towards that thing, that cloud of—

The mist quivered, expanded, then shot for Djola, enveloping him. It churned and churned like a small storm, until finally dissipating, and Djola was left standing.

". . . Djola?" asked Ashâke.

Djola looked at her, and she did not see anything she recognised there.

"RUN!" screamed Iyalawo. "GO! GO! GO!"

She fled. Behind her came the sounds of her mother and Yaruddin engaging in battle. Yaruddin, wearing Djola's skin. Djola was . . . was he dead? Or was he simply possessed? Was that how the followers moved about, then? Taking people's bodies so one could never know if the person before you was really who they seemed to be? That was a terrifying notion. There was so much she didn't know, so much she wasn't prepared for, and—

Ashâke stumbled out of the forest and into the camp.

"No," she gasped.

The boats were ablaze. They burned, consumed by unnatural purple flames, thick black smoke billowing into the morning sky as though from the mouth of a bronze forge. Even as Ashâke watched, the largest boat exploded, pieces of wood flying everywhere. With an earthy groan the ruined carcass of the boat began to sink into the boiling river.

"No."

Pandemonium reigned: griots raced about, screaming, yelling, wailing at the top of their lungs. Tents were on fire, half-buried in the mud. Clothes were strewn about, fluttering in the wind like birds. A large cauldron still squatted over a firepit, cooking a breakfast that would never be eaten. And on the riverbank . . .

"Stars above, please . . . no . . ."

The riverbank was littered with bodies, some lying face down, some lying face up, all of them unmoving, as if they'd simply collapsed where they stood.

Ashâke stumbled for the nearest cluster of wailing griots. At the centre was a woman, or what used to be a woman; now she was . . . her skin had the texture of glazed terra-cotta, riddled with cracks. Alabaster white, from the braids of her hair to the clothes she wore, she looked like a sculptor's impression of a woman, rendered in clay and fired in the kiln, as though she hadn't once lived and laughed and drawn breath, as though she hadn't once dreamed and loved and hoped for the future. Where her eyes should be were sunken holes, smoking faintly. Ashâke realised with a pang that she knew the woman: Modupe, who'd served her a second helping of porridge the night before, her newborn strapped to her back; Modupe, who'd japed that her husband was prone to nighttime flatulence. Now she was dead, *dead*.

"What happened?" Ashâke croaked. But she knew what had happened. Yaruddin had happened.

No one paid her any mind, as consumed by grief as they were, and Ashâke found herself muttering empty words of comfort, barely registering the words she spoke. Her eyes fell on a figure close to the river and she was running, breath catching in her throat, pain catching in her heart. She slipped in the mud, fell, and rose again.

"AH!" The word tore out her throat in a gasp of anguish.

Mama Agba half knelt, half sat on her haunches, arms raised as if to shield herself. Frozen on her face was a haunting expression of agony, her mouth opened in an endless, silent scream.

A wounded cry escaped Ashâke's throat. She knelt there, beating at her chest, as if to wrench the pain from it. Not Mama Agba. Please, not her too . . .

Baale Jaha knelt beside his wife, covered in mud and soot, his hair half-singed off his scalp. He looked so small, so diminished, a far cry from the proud Master Griot who had Sung to her mere hours ago of the Fall. He held Mama Agba's calcified hand in his, gazing at nothing in particular, a lost expression on his face, as though he couldn't quite believe any of this was real. Ashâke couldn't blame him; *she* was finding it hard to believe any of this was real, that this wasn't some hideous nightmare conjured by the barrage of revelations she'd had over the last few hours.

Baale Jaha's bloodshot eyes slid towards her, as if only just noticing she was there. They trailed over the etchings on her skin, the ancient glyphs binding the orisha within her. Ashâke saw the moment comprehension dawned on him, his eyes hardening with the weight of understanding. *"You,"* he whispered, stabbing a trembling finger in her direction. "They were looking for *you*."

"I'm sorry," she gabbled. "I'm so sorry—I didn't know—"

But he wasn't listening to her. "I didn't understand, but . . . Bahl'ul's followers. They came . . ." His face contorted in fury as he took in the carnage around. "They're all dead . . . because of you!"

"No . . . I didn't mean for all this . . . I didn't know. I'm sorry!"

Ashâke looked around at the countless dead griots. Baale Jaha was right. This *was* her fault. If she hadn't left the temple they never would have found her. If she hadn't attempted to bind an orisha they wouldn't have known where she hid in the first place. And now, because of her, scores of his people were dead, countless children orphaned.

She pushed to her feet and ran, slipping in the mud, wiping snot and tears from her face. As she breezed past, her eyes fell on Ralia, sobbing over the lifeless form of her father, beating at his chest. "Wake up, baba! Wake up!" When the girl saw Ashâke, she ran towards her, crashing into her and burying her face into Ashâke's belly as she bawled, "They killed my baba! He is dead!"

Ashâke found herself at a loss for words. How could she comfort Ralia when she was the cause of her distress? So she simply stood there and held her as she sobbed.

That's when she saw them.

First, she saw a woman striding towards her, her eyes pinned on Ashâke. On the left, cutting diagonally through the camp, a man. Ashâke turned around and saw Iyalawo striding out of the trees, a blade at her hand.

The fight drained from her. Her mother was dead, her body stolen. But what had she been thinking? They never stood a chance. How could you kill one who simply leapt into your body? How could you kill one who laid waste to the orisha themselves? You couldn't. And the orisha. Where were they when she needed them? Silent as usual.

The three followers spread out, predators slowly encircling their prey. There was no escape for her. Not that Ashâke intended to escape.

She pried Ralia's arms from around her waist and pushed her away.

"What are you doing?" cried the girl.

"I'm giving myself over. They won't stop until they have me."

"You promised." Ralia's lips trembled as fresh tears poured down her dirty cheeks. "You promised not to leave."

At that moment, Baale Jaha bellowed out a high, anguished note. Sonorous, it carried through the smoke-filled air, over the trees and across the river to the mountains of the east, which cast it back in a long, drawn-out echo. At first Ashâke thought it a wail of grief, harrowing in its starkness. But as the mountains replicated the single, wavering melody, she recognised it for what it was: the beginnings of a Song. One by one the griots, scattered across the length of the beach, hurt, wounded, tearful, took up the Song. They Sang without koras or flutes or drums. They Sang without embellishment or ceremony. There was only their voices, blended as one in grief, in pain, in defiance.

The world dissolved. Away fell the riverbank littered with bodies, away fell the boiling river and the burning boats. Ashâke felt the magic of their Singing as she was sucked into the depths of a Memory.

They stood in a market beneath a blazing sun. By the golden pyramids in the distance, gleaming in the noonday sun, she guessed it was the oba's market. Ashâke looked down to find herself standing behind a stall of oranges and papaya, dressed in trader's clothes. Gone were her etchings; in their place were tattoos, loose whorls inked in Kongi blue.

They were in the Middle Belt, although in which kingdom she could not tell.

She moved, staggering through the crowd. The griots' Song filled the air, filled her head so that she heard it even over the chatter of the market, over the cacophony of a dozen languages. She ducked through the stalls, where she saw a young Tessini girl crouched beside a tower of baskets.

"Ralia!" hissed Ashâke.

The girl turned to look at her.

"What's happening?"

"I don't know."

"What Memory is this?"

Ralia frowned, thinking. "The Stampede of Nok."

"A stampede?" she cried, alarmed. "But why would they . . ."

And then it hit her. They were trying to create a diversion. As she'd experienced, the griots did not simply re-create events, but placed you there, so you became a living, active player in a recollection. As it was, she found it hard to tell a living person from one conjured by Song. And she suspected Bahl'ul's followers were having the same trouble too; they could go through the entire market without finding her.

She heard the Master Griot, his voice booming through the air:

> *"On the first day of harvest in the Kingdom of Nok."*

She took Ralia by the arm. "Come," she said. "Let us go."

They ducked through the stalls, past haggling traders

and haggling buyers. Past a little boy wheeling a towering cart of sweet melons.

"In the oba's market in the shadow of the palace,
Did come peoples of the kingdoms, from Nago to Skaggás."

Ashâke found herself breathing fast, nearly sick with fear as her eyes flitted through the sea of faces—a Tessini man displaying bronze statuettes, an Ijebu cane-weaver with his cane chairs and tables, Nago tradeswomen with their fine tie-dye fabrics. There were so many people. Milling and jostling and shoving. And any one of them could be a godkiller. She kept expecting a hand to snake out and grab her, a black blade to slide through her spine.

She saw a cobbler, hunched in front of his stall, his mouth moving as he punched his needle through the sole of a shoe. He looked up and they locked gazes. And though he was now slight of build and bald-headed, and though he wore a sweat-stained kaftan that hung like a boat sail off his frail form, Ashâke saw the man behind those eyes.

Baale Jaha.

"Come," said the Master Griot. "Quickly!"

Ashâke scooped up Ralia and went to him. He led them round the back to the grimy alcove, where he began to draw on the wall with chalk.

"What are you doing?" asked Ashâke.

Jaha had drawn what looked like a crude arch on the wall. "We will try to hold the enemy here as long as we can," he said, "or until they find us. Give you enough time to escape."

"Escape?"

"Go through the wall; it'll lead you out of this Memory. Back to the river." His gaze was inscrutable. "Save yourself."

Even after all she had done, all the pain and destruction she had brought with her, he was still willing to help her. "Why?"

He seemed to get her meaning. "The orisha are still alive. We've lived so long thinking it was not so. But they dwell in you."

"I'm sorry. I am so very sorry. You have to know I wouldn't willingly put you in danger. If I had—"

"Many are dead, yes. But death is fleeting. May they live a thousand lives."

"May they live a thousand lives," echoed Ralia, wiping her eyes. Ashâke mumbled the words too.

"Now go. Go!"

And before she could protest, the Master Griot shoved her into the wall and into darkness.

TEN

Ashâke sprawled face-first into mud.

She sprang to her feet, catching Ralia just as she came tumbling out of—

A vortex. That was what it looked like. A mass of churning dark clouds brought down to earth, it spanned nearly the whole length of the riverbank. Ashâke could almost make out shapes in the vortex, but she wasn't sure if it was her mind conjuring things, trying to make sense of the mass, or if it was scenes from the actual stampede. Either way the griots had bought her time and there was none to waste.

She turned around and saw children. There were about twenty-five of them, huddled together, eyes red from bawling. A couple still sniffled, faces stark with fear no child should know. There were some adults, too, those like her who were not Singers, who'd come to join the griots, who'd had nowhere to go and had been given a place amongst the griots.

They were all staring at her. Ashâke was all too aware at that moment of the etchings carved into every inch of her skin.

"I'm going to go," she said.

Ralia clung harder onto her. "You promised not to leave!"

"It's me they want. If I'm not here . . . they won't bother you."

"Is that so?" said a woman, bouncing her fussing baby. "Look around you. Did that stop them before?"

Ashâke licked her lips, looking at their haggard faces, feeling the weight of their expectant stares. It occurred to her that they were all waiting on her to do something. *Orisha, what do I do? Please, speak to me. I don't know what to do.*

Her gods were silent.

They could go to the temple. They would be safe there. After all, it had hidden her from the followers all these seasons. But she didn't know the way.

"We can't run fast enough. There are so many children—"

A child shrieked. A bloodcurdling sound that raked at her ears, and Ashâke whipped about instinctively, pushing Ralia behind her.

A Singer staggered out of the Memory, clutching at his chest. The space where he had been sealed shut like water rushing in to fill an empty spot. But it was open long enough for Ashâke to see the godkiller standing there, to see that terrible black scimitar. The Singer dropped to the ground, legs kicking. Then he began to calcify, the white creeping out from the wound in his chest, eating his skin like some malign disease, until he was a statue of alabaster white.

"Ashâke!" screamed Ralia.

She looked up to see a face rendered nearly featureless as it strained against the membrane of Memory.

"The boat!" someone said. "Look! Gaza's boat isn't burnt. If we catch the wind we can follow the river to where it flows fast. It'll take us out to the Endless Sea, and if we keep to the coast we can make it to Inysha. We'll be safe there."

Ashâke did not think the children would be safe anywhere, not while they were with her. But there was nothing else to be done.

If the godkillers found all the Singers, there was nothing to stop them from coming after Ashâke.

"Alright," she said. "We sail for Inysha if we can. Children, let's go!"

They raced for the boat, Ashâke carrying some of the younger ones. The river still boiled and the air was thick with smoke. Ashâke untethered the boat and the older lads raised the sail just as it drifted free. The boat pushed away from shore, bobbing on the water.

But there was no wind, and the sail hung limp, and the boat drifted on the river like a forlorn log of wood.

The vortex began to shrink, Singers falling out of the Memory and dropping like flies.

"Take the oars!" Ashâke screamed. "Everyone who can row, ROW!"

They scrambled for the oars and began to row. Her arms were on fire. Her wounded hand shrieked with pain as she rowed. The water fought her with every stroke, the roiling river turning the boat on the spot, spinning it like a cork.

A godkiller stepped out, wearing Baale Jaha's skin.

"Eyin Orisha," Ashâke muttered, on the verge of panic. "Help me!"

The other followers were free of the vortex now, and they stalked towards them, into the river, slowly wading towards the boat. A girl burst into tears, calling for her mama.

"Ogun! Shango!" Ashâke didn't even know which one of them was alive, which one of them dwelt in her. "*Please,* I need you!"

She could feel the orisha, feel their power. But it was like staring at a far-off fire on a cold night, knowing its heat will keep you warm, yet unable to get close enough to touch it—

Suddenly, a wave of nausea washed over Ashâke, and she shut her eyes to keep the dizziness at bay. Everything fell away: the heat from the burning boats, the acrid taste of fear in the back of her throat, the screams. When she opened her eyes, she found herself standing in a vast hall.

"What in the . . ." She patted every inch of her body to ascertain this was real. It was, at least, it felt so. But how had she come to be here?

Ashâke was suddenly aware of another presence, and she twirled around, coming face-to-face with a woman three paces from her. She stood, arms clasped behind her back as she watched Ashâke silently. What was most shocking was not the fact that she hadn't been there a moment ago; it was that she was Ashâke's replica, from the crown of her head to the glyphs cut deep into her skin.

"What is this?" breathed Ashâke, her heart racing. "Who are you?"

Her doppelganger frowned. "I am you."

"What . . . am I dreaming?"

"Does it matter? The more important question is, why are you here?"

"Why am I . . ." She looked around, still struggling to grasp what was happening. "I don't know, I was . . . I was on a boat—"

The woman turned and started away.

"Hey! Where are you going?"

Ashâke's footfalls pattered across the floor as she took off after the woman. And though her doppelganger strode without haste, Ashâke could not quite close the gap between them.

"You shouldn't run," said the doppelganger offhandedly as she vanished through a doorway.

Ashâke found her in a small chamber, standing before a massive brass disc that floated in the centre of the chamber. It looked like a giant puzzle piece, made up of several dozen smaller pieces interlocking one with the other to form the disc. At its very centre was a depression in the shape of a hand.

The woman turned at Ashâke's approach. "Why are you here?"

"I don't know!" said Ashâke, starting to get annoyed. She really did not have time for riddles. "But I have to get back, *do you understand*? The followers . . ." She trailed off.

The woman *was* her, which meant she must represent a manifestation of Ashâke's mind, trying to tell her something, trying to give her the answer she'd been searching for. "I'm here for the orisha," said Ashâke. "I . . . I need their help."

Finally, the woman smiled. "They have been waiting for us." She nodded at the disc. "Mother locked them away, but it is time for you to set them free."

"How?"

But she needn't have asked. The disc was a door, and she was the key. Taking a shaky breath, she lifted her hand and pressed it into the depression.

"I offer myself to you," she whispered. "Now and forever. Take me. Use me."

With a clicking sound the disc began to peel open, each plate retracting like the petals of a flower, until the disc was no longer a disc but a vast brass ring, a portal, a doorway, and beyond it she saw—

A searing golden light tore through the opening, engulfing Ashâke in its ethereal luminescence.

The screams told her that she was back on the boat. Ashâke opened her eyes, surprised to find she was still holding the oar. The followers were where she had last seen them, slowly making their way towards the boat. Time had frozen, it seemed, but now . . . *now* she was different.

Ashâke pushed aside the oar and rose to her feet.

She felt a stirring in her, a great opening as though her entire being were yawning agape. She was a vessel, a vast hollow vessel, and every vessel is made to be filled.

She felt the power rush into her, a great cascade of raw, unfettered energy. She saw her etchings come alive, blazing a bright white-blue as they writhed across her skin: the thousand names of Olodumare etched into her, His thousand aspects replicated in the orisha.

Ashâke was aware in a way she never had been before. She knew the bird that trilled in the air, the worm that burrowed in the deep of the earth; she knew the vast expanse of the Endless Sea, and the creatures that plumbed its fathomless depths. And she knew the wind, and its many names, and its many forms. She called forth the wind from the corners of the world, from the east and the west, from the north and the south. She called the wind by name.

And it answered.

A gentle breeze stirred the air. Chilly, like the first breeze that heralded rainfall. Overhead, birds shrieked as they flapped for safety. Then Ashâke heard the sound, a deep rumble that thrummed in her chest. The sky darkened, turning day to night. The earth shuddered as if in the throes of an earthquake, the trees rattled as if buffeted by a stampede, and the storm appeared round the bend.

A great black wall of churning wind: it dwarfed even the mountains, howling like a fiend from Apadi as it tore down the valley, tearing trees up by their roots, gobbling up mud and river and the still smouldering remains of the griots' boats. The river frothed, drawn into a great wave near seventy feet tall, so that what came was a fast-travelling wall of wind and water consuming everything in its path. Ashâke watched the followers turn, faces drawn in alarm as they tried to flee, and then they were sucked like gnats into the storm.

The boat began to rock dangerously, old wood groaning as it was buffeted again and again by the tumultuous waters. With a resounding crack a side plank tore off and spun fast into the wind. Screaming, the griots huddled amidships, clinging to each other for dear life as the boat spun.

Ashâke stood at the prow, arms lifted as if in prayer as she worked the wind. She could feel it, bursting with unbridled power as it charged at them. The boat would get sucked into the storm, ripped apart, everyone sent flying. She couldn't have that. She couldn't have them all perish. So she seized the storm by its heart and forced it to her will. And as the storm front hit them it parted, parted like river flowing around a boulder, so that they were in the middle, in a safe bubble, engulfed in its teeming raging darkness.

They were travelling downriver, moving fast for the Endless Sea. And she could feel it: the storm was still growing. She felt it straining against her control, fast slipping her grasp, and it took everything in her to hold on to it. Blood poured from her nostrils, hot and sticky. She tasted the iron tang of it as it leaked into her mouth, as she cried and strained with everything she had.

She was a vessel. A vast empty vessel. But she had taken too much too quickly, and she was overwhelmed.

A song pierced the air. It came from everywhere and from *within* her. A song both strange and familiar, it was the most beautiful thing she had ever heard. And as she listened it soothed her, washed away the pain and worry. Washed away the fear. And Ashâke *knew*, in that moment, that the weight was not so heavy to bear.

She felt someone take her by the hand, and she turned to find a woman holding her. A woman whose white hair billowed out in a halo, whose eyes were the colour of the Endless Sea, and Ashâke knew her as surely as she knew herself. For this was no woman.

I am here, said Yemoja.

Someone else took her other hand, and Ashâke turned to find the orisha of storms, whose countenance was that of the tempest, and whose smile shone with the light of a thousand suns.

I am here, said Oya.

And as three, as one, they lifted their hands to the skies.

ELEVEN

Ashâke stood by the window, watching the slow rise and fall of Ralia's chest as she slept. Behind her the sounds of Inysha filtered in: fast-paced chatter peppered with raucous laughter, the occasional hoot of a loon. Just across the street someone was hacking out a sorry tune on a kora. The city never slept, as Ashâke had come to learn; it thrummed with the constant hum of activity. She still found it strange to be among so many people, and she doubted if she'd ever get used to it. If it were up to her, she would remain here behind the walls of this house, safe from the world and everything in it.

It had taken them three days to reach Inysha, three days during which she had slipped in and out of consciousness as she communed with the orisha. It had seemed far shorter than that, and when she finally woke she felt different. She now felt the presence of the orisha constantly, heard their voices at will.

The other children were scattered about the room, snuggled in their mats. It reminded her, oddly, of her time in the temple. Where that had been an institution founded on secrets and obfuscation—however necessary they had been—here in this room amongst the children, there was only truth, and love, and hope. A braid slipped into Ralia's half-open mouth and Ashâke pulled it out gently and tucked it behind her ear. She hovered a moment over the girl, watching the crease between her brows as she dreamt. Then she kissed her on the forehead.

"Goodbye, little one," she whispered. She picked her way across the slumbering children and slipped out of the room.

"You're leaving."

Ireti sat in the rocking chair in the living room before an altar she'd erected to the dead griots. She was Mama Agba's younger sister, who had married a woodworker and given up the nomadic life to live with her husband in the city. Nearly a week had passed since Ashâke had come upon her door, twenty orphaned children in tow. The woman had sat silently as they regaled her with all that happened, telling her how an entire clan had been wiped out, that her son Djola and her sister were dead.

"Yes," said Ashâke. "I am leaving."

Ireti finally turned to look at her. Her likeness to Mama Agba was uncanny. She had the same silver-white hair, the same bushy eyebrows. Ashâke could almost pretend that this was Mama Agba, the kindly woman who had taken her into the fold, clothed her, fed her, cared for her. She could almost imagine that Mama Agba was here, instead of lying frozen on a riverbank in the forest. Almost.

"When Ralia wakes up . . ." said Ashâke. "You'll let her know?"

The woman nodded.

"I fear she won't forgive me. She'll think I've abandoned her."

"You'll be surprised how forgiving children can be," said Ireti. "In time she will come to understand. She is my daughter, now. They are all my children. I will take care of them."

Ashâke nodded, then turned to leave.

"Where will you go?"

"I do not know. Wherever the orisha direct me."

"Tell them . . ." Ireti took a deep breath. "Tell the orisha I will spread word far and wide to the sister clans. The world will know what has happened. The world will know of the sacrifice of my people, may they live a thousand lives. The world will know that the orisha yet live."

Ireti had spent the past few days thoroughly interrogating each child, asking them for every arcane bit of detail they could recall of the events that transpired. When she summoned the tenth child, Ashâke realised why: she was capturing the Memory. The woman might have abandoned the nomadic life, but she remained a griot—a Singer—and would tell this tale until it reached the ears of all who would listen. Her mother had said the priests had been fighting a war of belief against the followers of Bahl'ul. But they had not had the griots on their side.

Ashâke nodded. The path before her was uncertain and

filled with danger. But she was not alone. She would never be alone anymore.

With one last nod at Ireti, Ashâke opened the door and stepped out into the night.

EPILOGUE

Alone in the darkness, the Teacher knelt, unmoving.

He might have been deeply asleep, for his eyes were shut, the crinkles in the corners softened. He might have been in communion, for his breaths were deep and measured, eyes dancing beneath closed eyelids. But he was neither asleep nor in communion.

Before him lay a small pool, the water black and reflective in the low light. The Teacher opened his eyes and gazed into the fathomless depths as though searching for meaning, for purpose, for instruction. He studied his reflection for a long moment, then dipped a hand into the water and began to stir.

He moved his hand slowly, water sloshing and gurgling, until he worked the water into a whirlpool, and the blackness began to bleed like ink to the edges of the pool, until he stared into a clear water that became a window.

The Teacher looked.

He saw a river, its still waters filled with broken trees and debris. He saw the riverbank littered with several calcified bodies, hollow eyes staring sightlessly. He saw ruined hulls of charred boats, beached ashore like the carcass of some great Endless Sea beast. So much death. So much waste. There hadn't been such wanton destruction since the Fall, since he plunged his blade into the Supreme Father and freed man from the yoke of the orisha.

He sighed.

His children had strayed far from his teachings, made a mockery of his edicts. But then he had been gone for so long. Too long.

No matter. He was here now. The Guardian still eluded them, but he was here to set it all right. If something must be done well, one needs must do it oneself.

Slowly, the Teacher rose to his feet and went out into the world.

ACKNOWLEDGMENTS

While I wrote the words that make up the story you've just consumed, several colourful characters conspired to produce the book in your hands. Amongst them are agent extraordinaire Alexander Cochran, and my editors Jonathan Strahan (who I asked very nicely if he'd look at my drivel and who very nicely did not balk) and Eli Goldman (who has shown me nothing but gracious support and infectious enthusiasm since *Breathe FIYAH*). Thanks to Shawna Hampton for copy editing (I am forever in awe of copy editors and their superhuman attention to detail), Christine Foltzer for the impeccable art direction, Godwin Akpan for absolutely stellar cover art, and everyone at Tordotcom who worked tirelessly to bring this book to life. Thanks to Chinaza Eziaghighala, Somto Ihezue, Oluwatomiwa Ajeigbe, and Ephraim Orji, the first people to read this book who weren't contractually bound to be kind but were kind anyway.

ABOUT THE AUTHOR

Joyce Nkanor

TOBI OGUNDIRAN is the award-winning author of *Jackal, Jackal,* a collection of eighteen dark and fantastical tales. He has also been nominated for the British Science Fiction Association, Nommo, and Shirley Jackson Awards. His short fiction has been featured on the hit podcast *LeVar Burton Reads,* but also appears in journals such as *Lightspeed, The Magazine of Fantasy & Science Fiction, Beneath Ceaseless Skies,* and in several Year's Best anthologies. Born and raised in Nigeria, he now lives and works in the U.S. South.

tobiogundiran.com
@tobithedreamer
@tobi_thedreamer